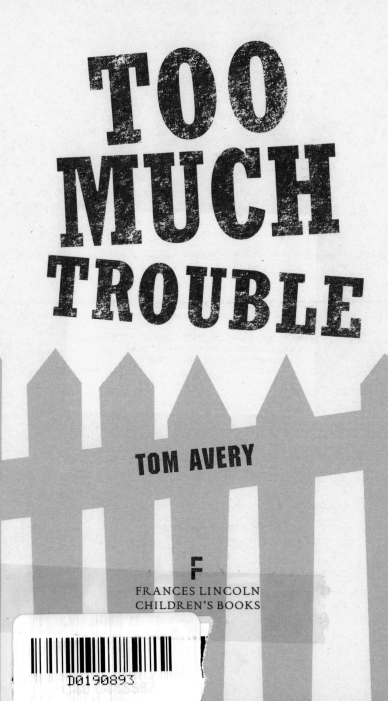

TOO MUCH TROUBLE

TOM AVERY

F

FRANCES LINCOLN
CHILDREN'S BOOKS

Prologue

The gun was much heavier than I expected. I struggled to hold it steady, two feet out in front of my face. Heavy, cold and terrible. I had seen several guns, hundreds if you count those in films and on television, but I had never held one. I had certainly never pointed a gun at someone's face. I had never threatened to take away a person's life.

'Give me the piece, Emmanuel,' said the large man without a trace of hesitancy, as I stared at his face through the sights of a pistol. His slow, accented drawl resounded with the sure confidence of a man who was used to obedience. 'Give it to me, boy!'

My hands shook as my resolve began to break.

Chapter 1

If you stay really still and really quiet, people don't notice you. Even if they're looking straight at you. Even if they're asking you questions. Even if you're answering them. I was good at not being noticed. No one had noticed me for years.

You can be too quiet. There's quiet and then there's 'weird quiet'. If you're weird quiet you definitely get noticed. I knew a boy called Akeeb Aslam, he was weird quiet. He got taken out of my class. After that he had to talk to Miss Harding every break-time about how he was feeling, and other stuff that teachers think pupils need to talk about. I didn't want that to happen to me.

If that had happened, the game would, almost certainly, have been up. If that had happened, people would have started asking the right questions, the kind of questions that could have caused trouble for more than just me.

This is not the story of how I stayed quiet, how I slipped under the radar of so many teachers. This is the story of questions being asked and trouble being encountered. It starts on my last day at my first secondary school; I was in Year Seven.

It starts here because I want you to see my last ordinary day before guns and threats and 'real' crime entered my life.

That day my geography teacher, Mr Banks, was asking us all where our families came from. We were meant to be learning about why people move to different countries. He called it migration. I knew all about migration.

He had asked a few pupils before me. Some from England, some from Pakistan. A lot of the pupils who went to that school were from Pakistan. A lot were from England too. Then it was my turn.

'Emmanuel,' Mr Banks said, 'could you tell the class where your family come from?'

Be quiet, but not too quiet, and never answer too

quickly either. Weird keen and weird quiet, they both get noticed.

After trying to look thoughtful, I replied, 'My mum's from France and my dad's from Central Africa, sir.'

'Wow! Where did you grow up, Emmanuel?'

'A bit in Africa and a bit here, sir.'

Mr Banks kept on going. 'Where do you call home then?'

I just shrugged.

'Thank you, Emmanuel,' Mr Banks said. Then he moved on to Billy. Billy's mum and dad were just from England. Mr Banks didn't say 'wow', but I'd rather my parents were from England.

I guess I could have said I was from anywhere. Portugal would have been cool; I could have said I had gone to school on the beach.

But lying is not really my thing. Generally you don't need to lie. It's so much easier to leave out bits of the truth than to add in lies.

***

I walked home with Asad and Ikram. They were brothers, twins in fact, and probably the smallest

Year Sevens in the whole school. They had lots of cousins all over the place though, so nobody messed with them.

'Don't stop it, pop it and lock it, never gonna stop, you can't stop me!'

Ikram's phone was blazing out the latest Lil' Legacy track. We were all trying to rap along. Everyone loved Lil' Legacy at my school: everyone who counted, anyway.

'What you doing this weekend then, Em?' asked Ikram. He emphasised my name by kicking a Coke can into the road. I watched the can sail off the pavement and jolt to a halt as it hit the wheel of a parked car on the other side of the road.

'Nothing much. Might head into town. Maybe play some football. What about you two?'

'Goin' to our cousins in Bradford, innit,' Asad replied. 'Yousef's gonna show us his new car. He's gonna be driving soon.' Asad mimed his cousin driving along, bopping his head to show the music playing and turning his head from side to side in challenge to the other imaginary motorists.

Ikram continued. 'Yeah, he thinks he's gonna be a bad-man then. But I reckon Uncle will have him back at college.' Asad's mime ended with him crashing the car – he jolted around as if he'd been electrocuted.

Asad and Ikram were easy to be friends with. They hardly ever asked big questions and they would do all the talking if I let them, which suited me fine. They didn't even know where I lived. They knew I had a little brother but I had taught him enough not to go shouting his mouth off. I thought I had taught him how to not be noticed too.

I left the two brothers at the gate of their house as usual. I could see their grandma twitching the heavy floral curtains. I knew that if I hung around I'd get fed, but I had to pick up Prince, my brother. And besides, if you go to dinner at someone's house, they ask you questions and it causes trouble when you don't answer.

***

Prince used to walk home on his own, but the school had stopped him when he couldn't (maybe that should be wouldn't) tell them how far it was to his house. I had been picking him up for a few weeks and I did not like it at all. I walked through the gates of the playground just as the bell went. Parents as far as the eye could see, all waiting for their kids. I said hello to a few people, parents of friends and parents of Prince's friends. I never stopped to talk if I could help it.

'Emmanuel!' I heard a call behind me. I turned round to see a lady approaching me. Someone's mother, maybe Prince's friend, Harry's. 'Hello, honey, is your mum around?'

I looked to each side. Wasn't it clear that my mother wasn't around? 'Sorry, she's at home,' I replied.

The lady reached into her bag and pulled out a little slip of paper. She handed it to me as she said, 'Could you get her to give me a call, honey? We wanted to see what day Prince could come over for tea.' The piece of paper had a phone number on it and a name, 'Judy'.

'All right,' I said, as I pocketed Judy's phone number.

***

I had gone to St Mary's Primary School, now Prince's school, for just under three years. I joined near the beginning of Year Four.

It's much harder not to be noticed at primary school

than at secondary. You have one teacher all the time who tries to get to know the whole class. Then there's dinner ladies and teaching assistants and old ladies who just come in to hear you read, all keen on asking the 'cute little kids' questions. It's definitely harder at primary school, and I admired the way Prince did it.

He shone so bright that no one could see the boy underneath. He was one of the school's 'most promising' pupils; he was in the football and hockey teams; and, if anyone had taken him, he could have taken part in a national athletics competition.

I found it much harder than Prince. Teachers tried to call home four times about my behaviour. I learned quite early on, that to get by you sometimes have to do things that are 'unacceptable'. And 'unacceptable' behaviour sometimes led to fights: fights in which my temper always got the better of me.

When teachers phoned the number they had on my record, they only ever got an answer-phone. It was my uncle's answer-phone, and he was almost never at home.

'Why don't we have any other contact numbers for you, Emmanuel?'

I'd shrug, looking down at the floor. For some reason the teachers liked you to look at them when they were telling you off, even though this often made them angrier. I always tried to steer clear of the angry teachers, because my temper would only get the better of me too and, worse than anything, teachers hate you answering back.

'Well, do you know your parents' work numbers?' the teacher would continue.

I would shrug again. Shrugging makes teachers angry, but not as angry as not answering and certainly not as angry as lying - just the right amount of angry. The kind of angry where they are ready to give up on you, which was fine by me.

'You don't know any other phone numbers? Emmanuel, you are in Year Five now, you're not in Reception. You need to take some responsibility!' At this point the teacher's voice would be rising.
Whatever you do, do not answer. Glance up at them, looking as sorry as you can, then look back down. This is the best teacher-calming move I know.

Luckily, some teachers let it drop. They'd phone just that once, maybe leave a message, maybe write a note in my planner, maybe ask me about it the next day. They usually wouldn't even notice if no response came back – they had dealt with the situation.

Prince just got the regular letters home. Events, days out, school fetes, you know, the usual. Anything that needed signing, I'd sign. I signed as Victor Anatole. That's our uncle's name. I signed my own letters too. Like I said, teachers usually aren't that careful. I'd even signed Emmanuel Anatole on a few letters, when I'd not really been thinking. As long as they have a signature in their hands most teachers don't mind.

Looking back now, I know that the teachers must have been asking some questions. I'm sure that they discussed the two boys whose parents never showed up to parents' evenings. But no one asked the right questions.

There were teachers who really tried to care for me and Prince. Asking us how we were getting on. Asking about life at home. Asking about our parents. But I guess it's difficult to carry on caring when all you get is shrugs in reply.

Chapter 2

I could see Prince, standing with his class on the steps outside Mrs Jacobs' classroom. He hadn't seen me, but I didn't wave. I usually just waited. I didn't go over to the class because Mrs Jacobs would ask me how I was getting on at secondary school. I didn't really know how I was getting on. OK, I thought.

Eventually Prince saw me and pointed me out to Mrs Jacobs. She waved and sent Prince running towards me, his book-bag flailing over one shoulder and a piece of paper, with what looked like straws stuck to it, clutched in his hand.

'Yes, yes, yes!' he shouted at me. 'Can we get McDonalds, um-um?' He licked his lips as he said this and I remembered my own hunger. So far that day I had eaten a packet of crisps on the way to school and a slice of pizza from the school canteen at lunch.

I didn't reply, but asked, 'What is that?' And I pointed to the paper-and-straw construction, which was mostly green and held together with a lot of sellotape.

'It's a football pitch.' Prince held it up for me to inspect. 'Can't you see? We had to make a model of somewhere that makes us happy.' Prince was looking at his model, the look of pride in his achievement on his face battling with confusion about why I couldn't see what he saw. 'Most people just did their house and stuff. Miss said mine was very original.' He paused for a moment. 'I can't remember what she said 'original' meant. She thought it was good, anyway.'

I didn't think it was good. How can a place make you happy? It didn't look like a football pitch either. It looked like a piece of paper that had been painted green and had paper straws stuck to it, which is what it was. And that didn't make me happy either.

We didn't get McDonalds but walked home past Something Fishy, and got some dinner there. It was a bit of a longer walk, but well worth it - they did the best chips. We shared a large portion. I had a fish-cake and Prince had a battered sausage. Prince wanted scampi, but funds were running low.

In a sulk, Prince picked over his battered sausage and nearly threw a fit when I said, 'If you don't want it, I'll eat it.'

We walked down the alley between Kelfield Road and Greens Close. Near the end was our fence.

To get into the house we had to do some climbing. Our uncle had forbidden us to use the front door. He said we looked suspicious, and besides, he only gave us a key for the back. Prince loved the climb, but I didn't. Prince has always been better than me at anything physical, apart from fighting. No matter how many times we clambered over that fence I still felt giddy at the top of the wooden panels. I imagined what would happen if I fell off the top, what would happen to me if I was hospitalised, what would happen to Prince. Responsibility makes everything more dangerous.

We had to try to stay as low as possible while we climbed – we didn't want the neighbours to notice us hoisting ourselves over every day. First I helped Prince, and then I pulled myself up.

We used to have a loose panel that swung aside so we could squeeze through, but we wedged it shut when a massive dog got right into the house. We both hated dogs.

***

I had good reason to hate them. A Golden Retriever had tried to take a chunk out of my arm once. I know, a Golden Retriever! I was at the park, and Prince was at home. First I went on the swings. I always wanted to see if it was possible to swing right round, you know, over the top. Then I was just wandering around. Maybe I was waiting for one of my friends, I can't remember.

Anyway, this big stick came out of nowhere and whacked me on the side of the head. The stick wasn't so big that it knocked me down, but big enough that it really hurt. I was a bit dazed, but bent down to pick up the stick. Next thing I knew, this great big, hairy dog was all over me, teeth bared. It tried to grab my arm but just got my jacket, so I hit it with the stick.

Then this man came running over. He was quite old. He had dark hair streaked with grey and a big grey moustache that drooped over some of his mouth.

19

'What the hell do you think you are doing to my dog? Put that stick down, you little. . .!' And so on.

I just threw the stick, and when the dog followed it, I ran. I didn't look back. I was only nine then.

I think Prince hates dogs because I've told him that story so many times.

***

So we climbed over the fence into the most overgrown back garden you will ever see. The grass was so tall, Prince and I used to crawl through it and you couldn't see either of us. There was a bush about the size of a car that had taken over one side of the garden. Another plant had spread in and out of the grass. It had white flowers the size of my hand, that you could pop out of their leaves by squeezing the end.

We traversed that jungle twice a day, to and from the house. A very empty house. It had a mossy smell that hit you as you came through the door, like the smell of a garden crossed with the smell of an open dustbin on a warm day. All that the house contained was our mattresses, clothes, school stuff, a television and DVD player, and a lot of plants.

And I mean a lot. All identical, leafy plants.

The plants belonged to my uncle and his friends. They grew under special lights in the whole of the basement and the first floor. We lived on the ground floor. We were not allowed near the plants. Occasionally, we had ventured into the purple glow and warmth of the lights, and braved the intensity of the mossy smell that came from the leafy forest.

But we tried to obey my uncle as much as possible. We had discovered what happened when we didn't.

This is where we lived. Just me and Prince. We lived there alone because our mother and father sent us to England. We lived there because this was our uncle's way of looking after us. We had arrived in his life three years earlier. Giving us regular money and a roof over our heads was all that he said he could do. He also said that if we made too much trouble the money would stop and the plants would move into the downstairs as well.

I guess we made too much trouble.

Chapter 3

Our uncle Victor was a great man back in our country. I don't remember much from those days, when Prince and I lived in Africa, but I remember that people listened to my uncle. He would sometimes give talks in front of the whole town. He even had soldiers with him sometimes.

The last time I saw him there, I was eight. I was playing in the street, playing a game with stones that my father had taught me. You had to move the stones by jumping them over one another on a grid traced on to the ground. Seeing the dust of a big car coming, and hearing the noise of music over a rattling engine, I ran inside to my parents and Prince.

My father came outside, I stood in front of him and we both looked down the road as the car approached. I saw Victor and I shouted out excitedly, 'Uncle, it is Uncle!' I was little then and just saw a loving uncle, who occasionally brought us nuts and sweets.

'Hush!' my father said harshly. 'I want you to go and get your brother. I want you to take him out the back. And I want you to walk to school.'

I remember so clearly because it was in the evening and we had been at school all day. I remember thinking that my father was playing a joke on me. I remember that my father used to make jokes. But then I looked at his face. It was very serious. He looked neither angry nor sad, but somewhere in between.

I asked him slowly, 'You want me to take Prince to school?'

He said even more sharply, 'Now!'

I was stung. My father was normally so gentle. I looked down the road again and saw my uncle shielding his eyes from the sun and looking right at me.

In a moment I was back inside the house. I told Prince that I could beat him in a race to the school. Prince has always loved competitions. He was faster than me when he was just three and I was six.

'Slow-coach, slow-coach!' he used to chant, giggling. Anyway, Prince was out the back door as quickly as I came in the front. I followed him, my mind racing through thought after thought, trying to invent a plausible story for what my father had asked us to do.

'I will give you a head start of one minute,' I said to Prince. I was as scared as I had ever been but just as curious – and for a moment the curiosity had won out. By lingering for just sixty seconds, I thought I could try to work out what was going on.

I heard the rumbling vehicle stop in front of the house and the music cut off. I heard muffled voices and the front door open and close.

I heard my uncle's deep and almost sing-song voice. 'This is the last time I will tell you, brother, we can't stay here. The rebels are heading in this direction, it is not safe.'

'I knew you would go! But this is where we live. It was always just a playground to you, but we have built a home here!' my father roared back.

As his voice rose I could feel fear replacing everything else I had felt. I ran as fast as I could. For once I did beat Prince in a race.

***

On the night when this story starts, the night before our lives changed again, we watched the television and tried to do our homework. Prince had some maths work; multiplying two-and-three-digit numbers. I think I helped him but neither of us was completely sure. The worksheet said we had to write down all our working-out. We used a calculator, so we definitely got all the correct answers.

My English teacher had asked us to design a cover for a book we had been reading in class. I knew most people would do it on a computer. I did it in pencil and used all three of the felt-tip pens we had. It didn't look good. In fact, between my book cover and Prince's football pitch we had produced some work to rival Akeeb Aslam's at his most weird.

On the television we watched the usual soap operas, the ones that we had to watch in order to join in the right conversations the next day. We also watched a programme about a group of superheroes. They had to stop one of the baddies from killing his family. He was going around the country hunting everyone who was related to him, because he hadn't seen them since he was little. He was furious with them.

After that finished we went to bed. We pushed our

bags right up against the door of the room we slept in. None of our uncle's friends came to look after the plants that night. The bags wouldn't have stopped them, but they would have given us some warning.

***

So that is the day when this story begins. A day like many before it but not the ones that followed.

Chapter 4

When I turn eighteen I'm not going to have a big party. After all, it is just the same as any other birthday really. I don't know what I'll do. Maybe I will try to find the place that Prince had to make a model of, somewhere that makes me happy. That would be worth finding.

On Lil' Legacy's eighteenth birthday he did something stupid. He did something that, in its way, led to me holding a gun for the first time. I haven't decided whether I should thank him or not.

Like many mornings before, Prince and I left the house and crossed the garden on empty stomachs. The little money we had left was clinking in my trouser pocket as we clambered over the fence. This would buy us breakfast and stretch to a small meal in the evening. I was hoping Uncle Victor would visit us that evening. I hated to see Prince go hungry. Prince stopped being himself when he was hungry. He was no longer the fastest and smartest kid around. He became quiet when he was hungry. Weird quiet.

We stopped at the corner shop and bought four packets of Space Raiders crisps. I also got Prince a Chomp chewy bar for lunch-time, which should have kept him on form and out of trouble.

I don't remember seeing Lil' Legacy's face plastered across the front of the newspapers as we left the shop, but it must have been. Lil' Legacy could usually be found in one or more of the little papers, but that day he would have fronted them all. The little papers are the ones that mostly have their names in red and contain all the news that a twelve-year-old cares about. I know they are really called the tabloids, but I think they should just be called the little papers. 'Little papers' and 'big papers', then everyone would know what you are talking about and English teachers would have less to explain.

I walked Prince almost to his school. We parted

with a wave, and he set off running the last three hundred metres. If he got there too late the Year Sixes would have taken over the football pitch, and Prince and his friends from Year Five would have to play against the wall by the monkey bars.

***

Once I fell off those same monkey bars. Well, I'm sure I fell off loads of times, but one time I hurt myself really badly. Me and Chancey Mills were having a monkey bar battle. That is where two people start from either end of the bars, swing themselves towards the middle and then kick each other, trying to get their opponent to drop.

Chancey was really good - he gave the hardest kicks and had only been beaten a few times. I figured if I got him early, I would have a good chance. So, I set off really quick and swung really hard at him. I completely missed and my legs swung up in front of my face and then were flung back behind me. I lost my grip on the bars and came crashing down on to the concrete playground, hard. Really hard.

Some of the girls who had been watching started screaming out, and Mr Chiltern came running over.

I knew that I was hurt, but my fear outweighed my pain. What would happen if they called an ambulance and then couldn't get hold of any family? I thought a hospital would ask more questions than a school. Was this the kind of trouble my uncle didn't want?

I picked myself up, wincing from the shooting pains that were coming from my mouth and chest. 'I think I'm OK, sir,' I managed to say to Mr Chiltern.

'Are you sure, Emmanuel?' He lifted my hands towards his face and turned them over. 'Oh no,' he continued, inspecting my palms, which were streaked with reddish lines. 'I think these grazes are infected, we will have to amputate!'

He made a chopping motion down towards my hands and I managed to force a smile through the pain, which was making its way from my chest and round to my right side. I could also feel small bits of what felt like gravel in my mouth.

'Why don't you go and sit down on the benches for a bit, Emmanuel?' Mr Chiltern turned to Chancey. 'And I want to talk to *you*.'

'But, sir, I didn't even touch him! He just sort of had a spaz and fell right off,' I heard Chancey complain as I walked over to the benches.

It turned out that the bits of gravel were small

pieces of my front teeth. You'd recognise me even today by my chipped smile. I don't know what the pain in my chest was, but it felt the same for weeks. It felt even worse when I laughed or coughed or just took a deep breath.

I really didn't want to upset my uncle.

***

If you walk towards a school at the right time, you can see loads of families. Families walking. Families saying goodbye. Families hugging and kissing. Families arguing. Families sulking.

I always used to watch the families. It made me think of my old home. It made me think of my mother and father.

We used to do a lot of running with my father. We would run to school together. We'd run to the water pump. We'd run to Grandma's. We'd even run into town sometimes.

My father would run a few steps ahead of us and shout, 'Come on, slow-coaches.' Me and Prince would almost burst trying to catch him, giggling and panting the whole time. Sometimes we'd slow down so that my father would slow down, then we'd run as fast as we could. He would be watching over his shoulder though, and would speed up, laughing and calling out, 'You won't catch me like that.'

I was usually the first to stop, bent over and gasping for breath, but still smiling. As soon as I stopped my father would wheel around, run back to me and scoop me up.

'Well done, well done, Emmanuel. Next time. . .' he would say.

'We will catch you next time, Dadda,' me and Prince would reply.

My father would drop me on my feet and roar, 'Not if I catch you first!' Then we ran again, all of us laughing.

***

The best family to watch were Asad and Ikram's. More often than not I would stand by their gate, waiting and watching. I waited for Ikram to get all his stuff together and watched, through the living room window, his mum and his grandma turning over cushions and looking under chairs in search of a lost shoe, or keys, or a planner. Asad was normally ready and waited like me. He stood at the front door holding it ajar and hollering up the stairs. He shouted insults in Urdu that I didn't understand, directed at his less organised brother. They tried to teach me some Urdu, but I could never roll my 'r's enough.

Jee haa, that's all I remember. It means *yes*, I think.

Me, Asad and Ikram usually walked to school together, but something stopped me today.

They came tumbling down their path, having located Ikram's black-and-gold cap, which he had left on top of the fridge.

'All right, Em?' Ikram slurred through a mouthful of toast he was attempting to finish as he shrugged his bag on.

I nodded in reply, we all shook hands and bumped our shoulders together, a ritual greeting we had adopted.

'Can you believe it about Lil' Legacy?' said Asad as we began walking slowly towards school.

Ikram continued, 'It's proper big news, innit?'

'I didn't hear anything. What's happened?' I was slightly embarrassed. I tried hard to watch all the right programmes and hear all the news that allowed me to fit in, but I was completely lost on this one.

'You know it was his 18th birthday last week?'

I did know this, but listened intently to Asad's words. 'He had a massive party, right. . .'

Ikram picked up mid-sentence, 'and he must have got mashed and he was talking to loads of people and he told them that he was not meant to be living here and he had been illegal for years.'

My brain began ticking over very quickly as Asad finished the story. 'And now the police are after him and are going to deport him to Africa or somewhere!'

My brain was now spinning faster than it ever had, whirring through possibilities. Prince would definitely hear about this at school. Prince was a huge Lil' Legacy fan. Had I taught Prince enough to know what to keep to himself? Could I make it back to Prince's school before he went into class?

As I turned and began sprinting away from Asad and Ikram, I yelled a slightly incomprehensible excuse about forgetting something. I was followed by their confused laughter until I turned the corner at the end of their road. I pushed on full tilt, my lungs burning as my feet pounded against the pavement. I knew I couldn't keep up that pace for long, but thoughts still whirred through my head.

Images of my uncle angry. Images of Prince

being arrested. Ideas of what I could do if the worst had happened.

I tripped before my lungs gave out, and I was forced to stop. I skidded a good few metres along the paving but leapt up again in moments. I tried running but could only manage a hobble. My knee was grazed and bleeding, torn wet flesh showing through ragged holes in one trouser leg.

I found myself limping past parents on their way home from dropping off children. This was long before I got to the gates, and I knew I wouldn't get to Prince before he went inside. I still kept on going.

Chapter 5

I entered the playground as the last few Year Sixes followed their teacher inside the school. Heading towards the reception, I began formulating a reason why I needed to talk to Prince. I was going to be late picking him up? Or he had forgotten something? But I knew that Miss King, the receptionist, would say I could leave a message with her.

I was still trying to invent a plausible story that would get me a few minutes with Prince, as I pushed open the heavy glass door into the school.

Behind the long reception desk stood Mrs Marshall, the headteacher, beside a frowning Miss King, who had a phone receiver held between her cheek and her shoulder and was staring intently at her computer screen. They both looked up as I entered.

'Ha!' exclaimed Mrs Marshall. 'Speak of the devil! Hello, Emmanuel. We were just trying to call your parents.'

'Oh,' I replied, my thoughts thrown into turmoil by this revelation. 'Erm, can I just talk to Prince please?'

Mrs Marshall looked at me over her glasses. She wasn't cross, I think she looked confused.

'OK,' she said hesitantly. 'Follow me. It's probably best if you stay here till we get this sorted out.'

I felt my throat tightening and my stomach balling up as my fears began to be realised.

'Is everything OK, Miss?' I was not entirely sure what I was asking.

'You just come and wait with Prince and we'll see about getting hold of your parents.' I could tell Mrs Marshall was not going to tell me anything so I just followed. Every step felt heavier and I began to hear a humming noise that filled my head, blocking out thoughts that I didn't want to think.

Mrs Marshall led me to the first-aid room. Prince was sitting on the long, orange bed; one of the teaching assistants was crouching in front of him and cleaning his hand, her pale skin against his dark brown.

'You're OK, bub,' she said to Prince, inspecting his cut hand.

I hope we're OK, I thought.

The teaching assistant straightened up from tending to Prince's bloody knuckles and noticed us entering. She broke into a smile. 'Hello, Emmanuel, what are you doing here?'

I didn't answer but glared at Prince, who was looking at his knuckle and wincing.

Mrs Marshall brushed past me and I could hear her talking softly to the teaching assistant. I was intent on Prince and didn't hear what was said until the beaming teaching assistant spoke up.

'OK,' she said, still grinning widely. 'Leave it to me.' Then she addressed me and Prince. 'I'll see you boys in a minute. Keep pressing that pack against your hand,' she said, motioning to the vivid blue packet that Prince held in his undamaged hand.

Mrs Marshall and the happy teaching assistant turned and left. I could hear them speaking over footsteps that clicked along the wooden floor as they made their way back to the reception area.

I turned on my brother. 'What have you said?'

'I'm sorry!' was all Prince replied.

I quickly repeated myself, taking hold of Prince's shoulder. 'What have you said?'

He looked up at me from a further inspection of his knuckle. 'Nothing! I haven't said anything much.' He stopped for a moment and I continued to glare at him. 'Well, just, you've heard about Lil' Legacy, right?'

I nodded, my heart beating a heavy rhythm inside my chest.

'Well, I just told Gary Coomber that me and Lil' Legacy could be related. I told him I wasn't meant to be here too and maybe we were from the same place. You don't know; we could be like cousins or something.'

I looked at my brother and felt like I was seeing an enemy. I was so angry. I grabbed his grazed hand. He winced but I didn't let go.

He went on. 'Gary said he would tell on me and I'd have to go back where I came from. We got in a big fight and then Mrs Marshall came out. That's it. I promise. Like I said, nothing.' Prince finished with a whine as he finally managed to wrestle his hand free of mine and re-apply the blue pack.

A swear word began to form on my lips, but instead I blurted out, 'You don't get it, do you?'

Prince didn't answer. His eyes flicked down to his hand.

I looked up at the clock. I didn't need to know the time, but I couldn't bear to look at Prince. I pulled him up to his feet from the orange bed.

'Come on!' I said. I picked up his bag and headed for the door.

Chapter 6

'You look after him, Emmanuel.' Those were the last words I heard my father say.

It was on my last day in Africa. A very long day. I remember being woken up by my mother. She held out a cup of hot porridge to me and told me to eat and get dressed. Then she fussed over Prince. He was still so little at six years old.

When I was dressed my father came inside, and a man, whose face I knew but whose name I didn't, came in behind him.

'This is Mr Ekpo, Emmanuel,' my dad said, smiling at me. 'Say hello. He is going to help us.'

I said hello shyly. Mr Ekpo was a vast man and his

face was set grimly, as I had seen it before. He didn't look angry but his face was far from friendly.

'Is the little man ready, my love?' my father called past me to my mother, who was encouraging Prince to eat.

My mother looked up and nodded. I thought I could see tears blossoming in her large eyes; eyes that were normally crinkled in a smile.

'OK,' my father went on. 'Emmanuel, I need to speak to you.' He took me by the hand and led me out of our one-room house. He called over his shoulder as we left, 'Please, Mr Ekpo, have a seat. My wife will get you a drink.'

Outside it was as hot as ever, the sun beating down on our heads and reflecting up from the dusty ground. A car was parked in front of our house. The first car I had seen for months. The first car I had seen since my uncle had left. It was a brown, battered jeep, with a small flag emblazoned in chipped paint on the driver's door.

'This is hard,' my father said, 'and I want you to listen carefully until I am finished. You understand, Emmanuel?'

I nodded and replied, 'Yes, Dadda.'

'You ask me why you don't go to school, and Prince

always asks when we can go into town. I can tell you, Emmanuel, because you are getting big now, that it is not safe, and your mother and I, we want you to be safe. You understand?'

I didn't understand, but I nodded again and said nothing.

'You and Prince are going to see my brother. Victor will look after you.'

For a moment I was excited at the thought of an adventure coupled with seeing my uncle. Then I realised my father hadn't included himself or my mother in his explanations. 'You're coming?' I said, my voice cracking slightly.

'Emmanuel.' My father looked at me, his glistening eyes a mirror of my mother's. 'Take this. It is all I have to give you.' He handed me a worn, brown envelope.

I turned it over carefully.

My father took it back and pulled out the contents item by item. A very small wedge of notes. 'Enough to buy something to eat,' he said. A slip of paper with a phone number and address, those of my uncle Victor. And two tickets, one for me and one for Prince. Tickets for the plane that would deliver us to the safety my uncle would offer.

He stuffed them back into the envelope, and

pressed it into my hand as Prince came running outside, followed by Mr Ekpo, and finally my mother, carrying my canvas school-bag.

'We are going to town, we are going to town!' Prince hollered at me, beaming.

I looked at my father, who gave me a pointed look.

My mother came over and gave me the bag. It was fuller than I'd ever packed it for school, the broken strap wrapped around it tightly.

'Tell your uncle that he was right,' my mother whispered into my ear. 'You tell him that your dadda said he was right.' She gave me a quick hug and went over to Prince.

Mr Ekpo had climbed into the jeep and was clearly waiting for us. My father took me by the shoulder and led me over to the passenger door.

'You will be gone when I return?' Mr Ekpo asked my father.

'Yes, yes!' my father replied impatiently, and then addressed me. 'You look after your brother, OK? You look after him, Emmanuel.'

So I did. I looked after Prince.

Chapter 7

It wasn't hard to get out of the school building. I looked up and down the corridor to check that no one was coming. I hadn't seen where Mrs Marshall and the teaching assistant had gone. When I was sure there was no one around, we headed for the nearest fire escape.

The difficult part was getting through the school gates. By this time all the parents would be long gone and the gates would be sealed. If you had a teacher's pass, the gates would open for you. Otherwise you had to press a button and ask the receptionist, Miss King, to let you through. I didn't think that Miss King would be too keen to see me and Prince strolling out. Our only chance was if someone was passing through just as we arrived at the gates. Someone trusting enough to let us out without asking questions, or gullible enough to believe any story we told them.

I walked quickly across the corner of the playground leading from our fire exit to the main gates. I longed for a passer-by as we walked. Prince hurried to keep up, still pressing the blue ice-pack against his swollen and bleeding fist.

'Where you off to then, boys?' The heavily accented voice stopped us dead in our tracks. My heart froze in my chest. I turned to see Dave Williams, the school's caretaker, walking towards us carrying a long length of wood over one shoulder.

'Er, doctor's, sir,' I said hesitantly.

'Er, doctor's? What you got, an 'er' cold?' Dave cracked a broad smile at us both, then started at our grave expressions. 'Oh, you must be very ill. I never see you without a smile, Prince.' At this, he walked on past us. 'Come on then, boys.'

My heart stuttered back to life and breath returned to my lungs.

'Thanks, Mr Williams,' I voiced, and Prince smiled weakly as the caretaker pressed his pass against the sensor. He pulled the gate open as a voice crackled over his walkie-talkie.

'Hello, Dave?' Miss King's voice was clearly strained and I could feel our luck ebbing away.

'What's up, Judy? I'm just down by the gates.'

I grabbed Prince's arm and hurried through the open gate, putting ourselves the other side of the black metal bars that surrounded the school.

'Come on, Prince,' I hissed and broke into a trot.

I could hear the conversation continuing over Mr Williams' radio as our trot became a run and in a few steps, an all-out sprint. As we reached the end of the short stretch of road that the gates stood on, we heard the caretaker's voice pursuing us.

'Hey, you two, what are you playing at? Get back here!' Dave was a big guy, not huge, but big enough and slow enough that we weren't scared he was going to catch us. I'm not sure what we were actually scared of, but I know that every step I took in that frantic dash was fuelled by fear.

For the second time that day I ran until my legs or my lungs gave out. This time it was my lungs. We found ourselves sandwiched between a tall, garden fence, a gate set in it every four or five metres, and the backs of what I guessed were garages.

I crouched on the pebble-strewn path, my body screaming for rest. I had thrown our bags down and the contents of one had spilt out. Prince leant against a fence, his hands on his knees, the ice-pack long since discarded, and his head down.

'What. . . are. . . we. . . doing?' Gasped breaths punctuated Prince's question as he tried to re-fill his lungs.

I didn't answer for ages. I collapsed further on to the path, my head resting on one of Prince's school books. I looked up at Prince before I answered.

'I don't know what we're doing, but I do know that they weren't about to drop that one. Mrs Marshall was gonna keep going until Uncle Victor turned up. Did you want to hang around for that?'

Prince looked down at me, then up at the top of the fence. He didn't answer my question but asked, 'Do you know where we are?'

I had no idea. We walked back to the end of the alley and looked for a road name. Gillott Road. We still had no idea where we were. We could have been on any one of a hundred roads around our area. We turned round again and followed the alley to the other end. It came out on to another road that we didn't know, Lords Lane.

We had no intention of retracing our steps, we didn't know who might be searching for us, so we took some aimless turns, hoping to find something familiar.

After about fifteen minutes of wandering we found one of the entrances to the park. As we went through the gate I pulled out the loose change, all the money we had in the world, from my jacket pocket. Prince ran ahead as I counted it slowly, down to the last penny. There was not enough.

Not enough for anything much.

I loved our park. In the middle was a huge, open space. A field of green, defined by white lines and football goals. It was pretty much on top of a hill, so it seemed like the sky went on forever. A concrete path ran all the way round the grassed area and paths led off this into the woods around it. One path led to a play-park, another to a BMX track, where me and Prince had often had foot races, jumping over the obstacles and charging up and down the ramps. We took another path to a smaller and more secluded field where the park-keeper rarely went.

This field was sloping and finished with a steep incline down to a row of trees that were perfect for climbing. Me and Prince picked the biggest tree.

We climbed until we thought no one would be able to see us from the ground.

Here we spent the rest of the school day. Neither of us mentioned the morning's events. Another thing we didn't mention was the fear that clung to us like the cling-film that covered Asad and Ikram's sandwiches every day - suffocating. The fear of what would happen if Prince's school did manage to contact my uncle. Of what would be awaiting us when we returned to the house.

We played boxes and hangman in the notes section of my school planner. We practised hanging from the branches by our ankles. We tried to climb to the highest branch. When we got hungry, Prince pulled out his Chomp and I had the rest of my Space Raiders.

We were still hungry, but we had both been hungrier before.

Chapter 8

My uncle gave us an allowance every month. It had been the same for the last two years. Sometimes he would bring us the money, sometimes it would be thrust at us by one of his friends. For the first few months, the money ran out before my uncle appeared again. I didn't know how to ration then.

For those weeks we lived on anything we could scavenge. That was hungry. I learnt about rationing pretty quickly after that.

It wasn't too bad during the week. We would sneak into the free dinners' queue at school. The weekends left us with fewer options.

I remember one Saturday. We were starving. We had not been in England long, and had not smelt the scent of a barbecue before, as it wafted through the air from a neighbouring garden. We didn't recognise the smell, but it still made our mouths water and our stomachs ache.

We sniffed the air around us, and licked our lips.

'Can I have some of that?' Prince asked. Prince's adjustment to our new life had been quick, but he still expected to get what he wanted.

We went through the loose panel at the back of the garden, and made our way down the path, following the enticing smell. I gave Prince a bunk-up to look over each fence as we went.

'Yes, yes, yes!' he said, when we found the right garden. He dropped down and I scrambled up, gripping on to the top of the fence and placing my feet flat against the panel. At the far end of the garden there was a large man. He wore a cap and a checked, short-sleeved shirt. The lower half of his body was obscured by a smoking barbecue.

'Darling!' he shouted. 'Darling, can you get me a tray? This chicken's done.' He stood listening, facing the house. No reply came and he barked, 'Darling?'

He walked into the house, and without a

word to Prince I hauled myself over the fence.

I ran as fast as I could, and reached the barbecue, panting. Quickly I picked up as many chicken legs as I could carry. I tried not to scream as my knuckles were seared on the blackened metal bars. As I ran back down the garden, I thrust the sticky meat into my pockets. I slammed into the fence and again hurled myself over. I crashed into Prince as I fell down the other side.

That was the first thing I ever stole. It was terrifying.

***

It must have been nearly time for school to finish when we decided to head back to the house. We could hear the jingle of an ice-cream van at the nearest entrance to the park. It was a ten minute walk back to the house.

We decided to take a detour to the mini-supermarket on the green. We stretched our money carefully. A pack of six finger rolls, a big bag of nachos, some cheese slices, and a big bottle of cola pop. I had just silver coins left in my pocket. Prince wanted another Chomp or a Freddo, but I knew that a little money in my pocket was better than slightly fuller stomachs.

As we walked the few minutes from the shop to our own alley and garden fence, you could almost hear us not mentioning what might await us. When we arrived, we both looked over the fence cautiously. There was no sign of my uncle or any of his friends, no lights on, no windows open. We both let out long breaths. You might have thought we'd been holding them for the last hour.

Prince climbed first. I passed over our bags and shopping. I hauled myself over and followed Prince through the jungle to the back door.

We went through into the kitchen. Prince threw his bag down in the corner and I walked over to the cupboard which held our three chipped plates. We were hungry and tired. We would eat and then go to sleep. I was so tired that thoughts of what tomorrow would bring were muted and distant.

As I swung the cupboard door open I heard Prince begin to scream, and I knew that trouble had found us.

In a moment I felt something strike the back of my head. I collapsed into the cupboard door and then down on to the floor. The cupboard door came crashing on to my chest, having been pulled away from the unit. Prince's scream redoubled in my ears and then cut off abruptly as I tried to focus my swimming eyes.

Something struck me in the side and I heard my uncle growl, 'Get up, you!'

I felt myself being lifted off the ground, my enormous uncle picking me up in one hand as he held Prince by the neck in the other. 'What have you done, you stupid boys?' Before I could begin to answer, my uncle released me and then quickly struck another blow across my face.

This time I didn't stay on the ground for long. Prince was beginning to turn purple and I could hear soft, choking noises. I leapt up and grappled with my uncle's arm, plunging my teeth and nails into his muscled limb. That made him let go. I heard Prince gasp a breath as another blow swept across my face.

'Get out, Prince!' I coughed, struggling to rise. The back door clattered as Prince rushed through it, then my uncle's box-fresh, white trainers connected with my stomach. I stopped trying to get up and just fought for breath.

'Why am I getting phone calls to my house?' my

uncle roared, then kicked me again. 'Your sons have run away from the school, they say!' He imitated a lady's voice as he kicked me again. The kick turned me over to face him. 'You need to come and see us or we will come and see you, they say!' My uncle picked me up again and threw me on to a wooden chair, then took a step back as if to admire his handywork.

I looked over to the door and saw Prince peering in through the glass. I willed him not to come back in.

My uncle had turned away from me, letting out a long sigh. I tried to control my ragged breathing and my uncle turned back towards me.

'You are my brother's son, but I cannot look after you any more. Here...' he said, thrusting a wedge of notes at me. 'Now, get out. You will be gone before my friends come. You will not like what they will do when they find that you have brought trouble. Get out, Emmanuel, take your brother and go.'

With these words, my uncle headed for the door that led into the rest of the house, pulling a packet of cigarettes and a lighter from his pocket.

Prince opened the back door and looked at me, open-mouthed, the shock clear on his face.

He mumbled, 'I'll get the stuff.'

That was the last time we ever saw that house. I've never missed it.

Chapter 9

There had been four occasions, when my uncle brought us our allowance, that he had stayed to play with us. Just four in three years. Once he had brought us an old Playstation One. A scratched and chipped grey box with a circular lid. You pressed a button and the lid slowly raised so that you could insert games.

I knew it was nothing to boast about, compared to my friends' elaborate computer systems, but me and Prince had never owned anything like it. There was a game called Bust-a-Move. It was brilliant.

You had to shoot these different-coloured bubbles at other coloured bubbles and if you got them in a group of all the same colour then the bubbles exploded. OK, that doesn't sound too fantastic, but it was two-player.

My uncle held a cigarette between his lips as he challenged me and Prince to play against him. You had to destroy more bubbles than your opponent. We didn't beat him once.

Every time he beat us my uncle laughed and called us funny names. Me and Prince came up with tactics for how we could win, and he laughed even harder. It was a very good day.

The computer console didn't last long. Me and Prince played on it semi-constantly the week after my uncle had left us. We were trying to get good enough to beat him. We hoped that maybe he would stay the next time he came.

But one evening, when we weren't busy with the bubble game, one of my uncle's friends found us somewhere we shouldn't have been. We had been playing hide-and-seek. I was 'it' and Prince had decided to hide in one of the rooms with all the plants. I had gone in to find him when I heard the front door opening.

I froze in the doorway and Prince collided with me on his way out. We lay in a heap as footsteps approached. My uncle's friend grabbed us roughly and threw us back into our part of the house. He phoned my uncle. I could hear their conversation, my uncle's replies muted and indistinct.

When he hung up, the man who had found us picked up the playstation, placed it in the middle of the room and stamped on it several times. It didn't work after that and we were much more careful about where we were found.

***

When I had the opportunity to look in a mirror I saw why Prince had looked at me with such horror.

After my uncle kicked us out, Prince quickly gathered our few belongings, then led me stumbling out of the back door. We didn't climb the fence. Prince kicked out the loose panel. We wouldn't need to worry about dogs in the garden any more. At the end of the alley we turned left, towards town. After a few steps I stopped by a car and glanced at my reflection. The failing, evening light bounced off the tinted windows and my face was clearly reflected.

The left side of my face was purple and swollen like a giant plum. Blood was seeping from my nose and was visible between my teeth. There was a red line cut into my chin. I guessed that this last one was from where I had hit the cupboard door.

Prince had stopped with me as I inspected myself in the car window. I looked at him. He was shaking and his face was pale and drawn. I knew that I couldn't expect him to take the lead, but I had no idea what to do.

We started with the obvious. 'Come on, let's get some plasters,' I said.

The notes that my uncle had handed me were more than our usual allowance and more than my father had given us when he had sent us away, but it was still not a lot.

At the entrance to the chemist's, I handed Prince one of the notes and instructed him on exactly what to look for. I didn't go in. I didn't want to risk the chemist asking me too many questions. We had no one we could trust.

I looked through the glass, watching a shell-shocked Prince walking up and down the aisles. He disappeared behind a taller shelf and I tried my best to stop the blood dripping from my chin. I opened my school bag. Prince had stuffed it with some of our things. A few pens, our two favourite

DVDs (my uncle had given us one every couple of months), a few school books and, bundled up in the bottom, most of my clothes. I pulled out a white sock and pressed it against my chin.

I looked down at the sock. Slowly a red ring appeared at the bottom of my vision. The arc of blood continued down the sock. My chin was bleeding a lot.

Up and down the high street, shops were beginning to close. Shutters were coming down. Shop assistants were walking or cycling home. I watched a man walk towards the entrance to the train station as dozens of people came through the other way.

This set me thinking. We couldn't go back to the house, my uncle had made that clear. We couldn't go to either of our schools, they would only call my uncle. If anyone from our schools saw us, we could be in the same trouble.

By the time Prince came outside with the plasters, I had made a decision.

'Come on, Prince.' I picked up the bags, threw one to Prince and headed to the train station.

***

I bet you're wondering what our favourite DVDs were. You'll be surprised. Well, you'll be surprised at mine. Prince's favourite was a set of four *Sponge-Bob* episodes. That's OK for a nine-year-old, right?

Well, mine was *Finding Nemo*. When you're a twelve-year-old boy, you don't tell other twelve-year-old boys that your favourite film is a cartoon about a fish. But it always made me happy.

I loved the beginning, when Nemo's dad is really protective. He won't let him go out alone, or even to school. He just wants to be there all the time. And then when Nemo gets taken, his dad does everything to get him back.

I don't really like Nemo though, and you *should* like the main character. He makes me cross right at the beginning, when he doesn't do what his dad says.

But I like the blue fish. She's funny. She thinks she can talk to whales and she can't remember anything.

***

I've never had a problem remembering things. I can remember that day so clearly. The way the blood felt, soaking into the sock. The way the plasters kept peeling off my chin. An image of Prince, staring at his shoes as I spoke to the ticket man. He was still pale. He seemed little, even littler than he was, I mean.

The train tickets were a lot of money. We wouldn't have much left. They would take us into town, and then all the way to London. We could have gone anywhere, but we knew that there were a lot of people in London. It's much easier to be invisible when there are lots of people around. Much easier to hide. And besides, we'd never been to London before.

The man at the ticket booth looked at us both very strangely. I thought for a moment that he might not sell us the tickets, but he did. There was obviously no rule against selling tickets to blood-soaked children. He tapped away on his computer and then they came shooting out of a slot into his waiting hand.

He slid the tickets, and our change, under the glass screen. The train wasn't going to arrive for fifteen minutes. We wandered into the little shop attached to the waiting room.

We looked around slowly, happy for our minds to be distracted by the bright and familiar wrappers of crisps and chocolate bars. We'd left the food we'd bought earlier in the kitchen, but neither of us felt hungry.

We'd been in the shop for maybe a minute when

the woman behind the counter growled, "Are you planning on buying anything then, boys?" We both looked at her blankly, then at each other. In the end we bought a big bottle of cherry pop.

Ten minutes later we were boarding a train. We knew that in one hour and fifty-four minutes we'd be in London, but we had no idea where we might end up.

I like trains. I'm not one of those people who take pictures of them but I think they're great. Buses are too slow. They stop all the time for people to get on and then they wait at lights and get stuck in traffic. We used to get a bus into town sometimes and it would take about half an hour.

In half an hour on the train we were further from the house than we'd been in three years. The day's events seemed to travel back in time. They could have been months ago.

Have you seen that *Superman* film where the lady has died, so Superman flies around the world so fast that time goes backwards? It felt like that.

The further we travelled, picking up speed, the safer and happier we felt. Further from my uncle. Further from that house. Further from everything we knew.

Chapter 10

We arrived at the huge, London station late. It was getting really dark, but the station was lit as bright as daytime.

Lengths of green metal made a criss-crossing, arched pattern far above our heads. Hanging from this, on bars made from more metal, were signs. They made me think of bats with long, long legs. Like a cross between a giraffe and a bat, hanging from the ceiling.

Signs to the exits, signs to the platforms, signs to the toilets. We didn't follow any of the signs, but rather, followed our noses. As soon as we stepped off the train, we smelt the sugary scent of fast and fried food.

We had slept for the last half-hour of the journey and had woken hungry. We hadn't eaten since our small lunch in the park.

Prince walked behind me. His head was down. We entered the fast-food outlet, weaving through the hundreds of people who stood, walked and ran through the station, waiting for trains, waiting for loved ones, waiting to go home.

Prince seemed far from himself, a combination of fear, tiredness and hunger pulling him down. I knew that food would help, so I got a cheese-burger for myself, and a cheese-burger and chips for Prince. I got us both a tap water; that was free.

We sat on smooth, plastic chairs fixed to the floor, a table between them. They were outside the restaurant, but still within the vast station. Prince slid down until his chin was nearly resting on the table, whilst pushing chips into his mouth. After just a few mouthfuls he pulled himself up and greedily unwrapped his burger.

I had done all that I could to clean myself up, but my bruised and swollen face still drew looks from some of the people who swarmed through the station. There was a smart-looking, white man at the table next to ours. He was wearing a suit with a pink tie. He was eating some chips whilst tapping away on his mobile phone, and every so often he would glance sideways at my face. I think he looked worried.

His wallet was resting on the table. A thick leather wallet with two letters stamped into one corner, SD. I pulled out our remaining money and counted it carefully. I knew exactly what it would buy in the shops that we had used for the past three years. I also knew that, in our normal circumstances, this money could have kept us for almost a week. But these weren't our normal circumstances and we had nowhere to go.

I made a quick decision and found that I was prepared to steal far more than chicken legs. Unwrapping my own burger with one hand, I slowly worked the squashed box of plasters out of my trouser pocket with the other. As I leant forward to take a bite of my food I carefully threw the packet of plasters right by the suited man's feet. He looked up from his phone and then reached down to pick up the packet. My hand shot out and his wallet was in my pocket in a moment.

Prince stared at me wide-eyed, his burger halfway to his mouth, suspended in the air. He knew what our father would have said about stealing.

The man straightened up and handed me the packet. His fingertips brushed my open palm as he placed the plasters there and I wondered if he noticed how damp it was. My heart was racing and my face felt as if it had been in the sun all day.

'Thanks, mister,' I said quickly, then addressed Prince. 'Come on!'

At the same time the man said, 'Are you OK?'

I just nodded to him as I tried to stand up. I didn't know if my shaking legs would hold, but they seemed to be fine as me and Prince rose in unison.

'Hang on!' The man's voice burnt my ears and I felt his large hand close around my wrist. 'Have you..?' I turned to face him as he continued. 'You've nicked my wallet!'

I had no energy and no words. I could sense Prince shuffling backwards, looking around for a place to run. I just stared at the man. He looked confused now as well as worried. He said, 'I think I'd better get the police.'

He held on to my wrist and looked around the station. His free hand reached for his phone and began to dial.

All the time my heart had been thumping harder and harder, and then it just stopped. A heavy hand was laid across my shoulder and a rough voice sounded from a metre above my head. 'Everything all right here?'

I looked down. Out of the corner of my eye I could see Prince staring at the person who had laid his hand on my shoulder. The voice continued in its heavy, London accent. 'Let go of my nephew's wrist and I'm sure we can sort this out.'

Nephew? That voice was definitely not my uncle's. One, it sounded nothing like him. Two, since when did my uncle stick up for us? No, that was not my uncle.

I finally looked up. I saw the underside of an unshaven, white face.

The man claiming to be my uncle carried on speaking before the wallet man could say anything. 'I know what you're thinking, white uncle, black nephew...s.' There was a pause before the s in nephews, as if he had just noticed Prince. 'They're my wife's sister's kids, and a right pain too.' He then addressed me, looking down at my confused expression. 'What have you been up to?'

***

Like I said, lying is not my thing, but I loved drama at school. Our drama teacher was the best. I've tried as hard as I can but I can't remember his name. He was still definitely the best, though. He really listened to everyone's ideas and he helped us make them better. I must have only had him about ten times before we left but I remember he used to say 'imagine' all the time. It was like his catch-phrase.

One lesson he brought this big box out and he asked us to imagine what was inside it. We all had to come up with ideas. I put a cap inside. Everyone at my school had a cap.

Someone suggested that the box contained a magic pen. We then had to think about why the pen might be magic. My group decided that whatever you wrote with the pen came true. Like if I wrote, 'Emmanuel Anatole lived in a little, quiet house by the beach', then that would happen.

The drama teacher loved that idea and he asked us to write what we would write if we had that pen. I wrote about that house by the beach. I didn't want Prince to live there, but every time I thought about him not living there I felt sick. So I wrote that Prince lived there too. I added some of the usual stuff too, like computer games and our own football pitch.

What I really wanted to write was 'and then Emmanuel lived happily ever after', but that felt a bit silly.

The drama teacher always said that I was really good at drama.

***

So I didn't lie, but I tried some drama with the man at the station. 'We haven't done anything, Uncle, this man just grabbed me.'

By this point the wallet man had let go of my wrist. He still looked worried but he also looked a bit scared.

The man pretending to be my uncle was grinning at him.

'These boys stole my wallet. It was right here, then they came along and it was gone.'

The large, rough-sounding man laughed. '*These boys* stole your wallet? They are a pain, but they're not thieves.'

The wallet man was turning a bit red. He said, 'Listen, I just know it was here before they sat down.' He pointed to the corner of the table where his wallet had been, then brandished his phone. 'I don't want to cause trouble but I think I'd better call the police.'

Then he pointed at my face and said, 'Is he all right?'

The man pretending to be my uncle looked down at me again. He ignored my swollen and plastered face. 'Right, boys,' he said. 'Empty out your pockets. This man thinks you might have taken something of his.' I looked at him pleadingly, but he just said, 'Go on, get on with it.'

Prince glanced at me and I nodded.

My little brother quickly pulled out the lining of his trouser pockets and the remains of the cherry pop label fluttered to the floor. Prince had spent at least fifteen minutes tearing it up on the train. He was going to dump it on the floor, but I thought a ticket inspector or someone might kick us off. He had nothing else in his pockets.

I emptied my left pocket on to the table, it contained the rest of our money in coins and a crumpled packet of plasters. I reached for my right pocket, the moment of truth. My hand plunged in and there was nothing there. I pulled out the lining and still nothing.

The wallet man looked as confused as I felt.

'I told you, mate, they're not thieves,' our pretend uncle said.

The wallet man looked behind him into the fast-food restaurant. 'Listen, I'm really sorry,' he said.

'I don't know. . . I guess I must have left it at the counter or something.'

'You'd better go and check, mate, anyone could have picked it up,' our pretend uncle said.

'Yeah, cheers.' The wallet man got up and hurried into the restaurant. As he did so, he glanced over his shoulder, looking at my face again.

The large, rough man said, 'Come on, boys, time to be gone.' He led us both through the station and out of the nearest exit.

Why did we follow him? What would you have done? 'Stranger danger' and all that. I guess we followed him because we had nothing else to do. I don't mean that we were just bored. We had nowhere to go, no one to see and nothing to do. And I guess we followed because he had helped us. For once I wasn't trying to look after Prince and me, someone had looked after us. He seemed pretty great.

He led us out of the nearest exit and kept on walking. He asked us our names and where we'd come from. He didn't ask about why we were on our own, but it felt like he knew all about us.

'Right, boys,' he said, 'my name is Mr Green. You can call me Mr Green.' He smiled at this, I don't know why.

Then he said, 'Do you want to do this properly?'

I didn't know what he was asking, but then he reached into his pocket and pulled out the wallet, the letters S.D. clearly visible.

'What?' I said, tapping my own pockets. Even though I knew that the wallet wasn't in there. 'How did you do that?'

He shrugged, then opened the wallet. He pulled at the contents and handed me two very crisp notes. 'So, do you want to do this properly?' he said again, tapping the wallet against his palm.

I looked at Prince. His mouth was open but then he looked at me and smiled. We were both smiling.

Mr Green really did seem great.

Chapter 11

It was about 10pm when we left the station. Mr Green said we had to hurry. He said he had some friends that he wanted us to meet. Friends like me and Prince. Friends that me and Prince would like.

When we went past another fast-food restaurant Mr Green replaced the burgers we hadn't finished, but then we hurried on. We got on a bus that took us over a long bridge.

Looking back, I guess it must have been London Bridge. At the time me and Prince had no idea. We were just marvelling at the sights. When we had got on the bus Mr Green led us up to the top deck. He pulled out his mobile phone, pressed a few buttons, and raised it to his head.

'Hello, mate,' he said into the handset. 'You got good news for me?' Mr Green got up and moved a few seats away from me and Prince.

We got off the bus about fifteen minutes after the bridge. Mr Green had put his phone away. 'Come on, boys, this is us,' he said. No one on the bus gave us a second look. We felt safe.

'Where are we going, Mr Green?' Prince said.

'Ah ha,' he replied. 'You'll soon see. It's somewhere where no one will come looking.' It was as if Mr Green knew exactly what we wanted to hear. After a few moments he carried on. 'Now, boys, you need to be nice to my friends and they'll be nice to you. They're all good. But some of them you need to be extra nice to. OK?'

I think I knew what he meant.

***

There was a boy at my secondary school that you had to be extra nice to. He was scary. Most of the time he was a right laugh and well funny in class. He would have failed terribly at trying not to be noticed. His name was Ryan.

Most of the fights that happened involved Ryan's friends, and everyone knew that there wouldn't have been a fight if Ryan hadn't set it up. He never got in trouble though.

Ryan was something of a king amongst his friends. They would have done anything he said. Maybe they were scared of him like everyone else was.

I remember one maths lesson. The teacher was at the board showing us something. Ryan picked up his friend's pencil case and threw it at a girl in the front row. It sailed past her and slapped against the white-board. The teacher turned round and stared at Ryan.

'What, sir? That wasn't me!'

'I'm not stupid, Ryan, pick it up,' the teacher said.

'But it wasn't me, sir!'

The teacher continued to stare at him.

I was sitting behind Ryan. The position where I was most likely not to be noticed. I saw Ryan kick his friend, whose pencil case it was.

His friend then quickly said, 'It was me, sir.'

The teacher looked at him sceptically. 'Come and pick it up then, Leo.'

As Ryan's friend Leo stood up, the teacher glared at Ryan, then turned back to the board. Ryan looked round, grinning.

I always gave Ryan sweets if I had them, and I let him or his friends copy work or sometimes just take my homework.

If Ryan had taken too much notice of me I would have been in even more trouble than if a teacher started noticing.

I knew who you had to be extra nice to.

***

We didn't walk for long before we arrived at a large, terraced house, maybe three storeys high with big, tall windows.

Mr Green said, 'Here we are.' He looked up and down the street and at the neighbours' windows, then walked up to the front door. We followed behind. At the door he pulled out a long piece of metal about the width of a piece of string and as long as a pencil.

He turned to us with raised eyebrows and said, 'Welcome to the madhouse.' He inserted the metal object into a lock and, after some skilful twisting, the door swung open. As soon as it opened we could hear Mr Green's friends.

Laughter. Shouting. Swearing. Every so often a smash of glass or porcelain. It sounded brilliant.

Mr Green closed the door behind us and led us

through the hallway and into a large room which was obviously someone's living room. But it looked like a dump. There was writing on the walls. Takeaway rubbish littered the floor. One of the sofas had a large rip in it, and the filling had spilled out.

Three boys stood on sofas and chairs around the room, bouncing up and down. A pile of crockery was on the floor beside one of the chairs. As we entered, the three boys were in the middle of a game of catch. Instead of a ball they were using a wine glass.

They erupted as we came in.

'Eh! Mr Green! Who's these newbies?' a little boy, who looked about eleven, shouted.

Another called 'Watch out!', and hurled the wine glass towards us. Prince dropped his bag and caught it by the stem. The bowl snapped off and smashed against the wall behind him. The three boys cheered.

Mr Green grinned and slapped Prince on the back. 'We've got a quick one here,' he said. 'Emmanuel, Prince, I want you to meet Ibby.' He was the little one. 'Kieran.' Kieran was really tall and a bit fat. He didn't look scary, but he was the biggest kid I've ever seen. 'And Jamal.' Jamal was the boy who threw the glass. He was about my size, but he held himself like he was bigger. He came over and shook our hands, looking us up and down.

'Go and get everyone.' Mr Green addressed this to Kieran and Ibby. 'What do you think, Jamal?'

Jamal took a step back still looking at us. 'I like 'em, Mr Green, especially this one,' he said, ruffling Prince's hair. I think I knew who I needed to be extra nice to.

Gradually the room filled up with more rowdy boys and a few girls. They were talking and calling to each other whilst they all had a good look at us. I tried to count them as they moved round the room and got to thirteen when Mr Green shouted, 'Shut up and sit down!' They all quietened down and found a place to sit, either on the floor or perched on a sofa or chair.

Mr Green waited for them to be quiet before he carried on. 'First of all, this is the last night here. We are moving tomorrow.' A few of the boys cheered and Jamal grinned wickedly. 'Make the most of it. Let's not leave anything valuable lying around. And secondly, you've noticed the new faces. This is Emmanuel and Prince, say hello to them.'

There was a range of replies, 'hello', 'all right', 'yeah, yeah' and other variations.

One girl just smiled at me. She was a really little,

white girl. She had dark hair and even darker eyes. She just smiled at me for a moment, and then looked up at Mr Green, who carried on speaking.

'Jamal, show them around. Everyone, be nice. I 'll see you tomorrow.' Mr Green acknowledged with a wave the various goodbyes that the kids called to him, then walked out of the room. The others began to disperse.

Jamal came and offered his hand again. He pulled us both to our feet and said, 'Right, let's make you feel at home.'

***

I just about remember moving with my parents to our first home. Before that we had lived with my grandma. My mother and father, me, and a little, baby Prince. I don't remember living there, but my parents told me that there wasn't room for all of us. Grandma had helped us find our own home.

It was tiny. Just one room. But I remember how happy my parents were. My father swung me around the room before we had any furniture.

It was a great place to live. We could walk to school and get the little green bus into town along the dust road. That was before I was big enough to run with my dad. My father worked at a factory. He rode his bike there, early every morning. Until the last few months.

The last few months we lived in Africa, we didn't go to school and my father didn't go to work. My parents didn't tell us why. We thought at first it must be a holiday.

After a while, though, we started to hear explosions and bangs in the night. Sometimes there was screaming. For the last few weeks we didn't leave the house much.

So I had been in a new house before, but not one like Mr Green had taken us to.

***

Jamal introduced us around. Like Mr Green had asked, everyone was nice. Jamal introduced Prince as the fastest little catcher around. Prince loved that.

We met everyone that night.

Jamal was sort of in charge. I was right about being extra nice to him. When he entered a room I could see the same look in people's eyes that I saw in Ryan's friends' eyes. Wary expectancy.

His main friends were Ibby, real name Ibrahim, Kieran, and two Jamaican boys called Michael and Dwayne. I made a note to be as nice to these boys as I was to Jamal. They all loved Prince. Michael and Dwayne called him 'the Little Prince'.

There were two girls who were inseparable. Carla and Sofina. They both had big hair and wore matching, green scarfs. They had other matching accessories that I saw on other days. They giggled when they met us.

There was also Alex, Sastre, Kammy, Julia and Freddie. I'm sure I'm forgetting some, but that was most of the gang. We met some of them playing football in the garden. Julia was a girl, but a bit of a boy too. I mean she was good at football and stuff.

The little, dark-haired girl who had smiled at me was called Terri. She was younger than me, maybe nearer Prince's age. She smiled at me again when Jamal introduced us. She didn't smile at Jamal, she didn't even look at him. She said hello quietly and then turned back to the book she had been reading.

As we left the bedroom, Jamal said, 'Terri's quiet. I think she's a bit messed up. You know?'

I didn't know, but I didn't ask either. Terri seemed all right to me.

Chapter 12

Do you remember your first day at school? I do. Not sure if you will get on with anyone. No idea where anything is. Trying to take everything in. And the utter exhaustion at the end.

That first night, with Jamal and Terri and everyone, was like that. Prince fitted in straight away but I felt nervous. Not knowing anyone. Not knowing where we were. Not knowing if we would be allowed to stay. But everyone seemed. . . well, you'll see.

After Jamal had shown us round, I played football for a bit. Sastre was the best. He could get over five hundred in keepie-uppy. All those guys were OK. They passed the ball to me and asked me some questions.

'Where do you come from?'

'Where did Mr Green meet you?'

'Why have *you* run away?'

I didn't like to answer too much. Habit, I guess. I didn't realise for a few days that all the kids shared similar stories. Trouble in their past. Runaways. Picked up by Mr Green. Brought to a house like this one.

When I got tired of football I thought I would go and try to talk to Terri. I walked through the lounge where Prince was playing crockery catch with Jamal and his friends. I walked through the middle of the room. Jamal threw a plate and I flinched as it sailed inches over my head. They all laughed. Prince laughed as well. The plate smashed into the wall as Dwayne failed to catch it.

Carla and Sofina were sitting on the stairs. 'All right, Emmanuel?' they chimed together, then giggled.

'I like your shoes,' Carla said, smirking. I looked down at my feet. I was wearing school shoes that I had bought at a supermarket. They were a year old and showed it. One of the heels was falling off and the laces were frayed. The many scuffs were highlighted by the thirty minutes I had spent playing football.

'Erm, thanks,' I said.

The two girls burst into giggles as I struggled past them up the stairs.

I knocked on the door to the bedroom Terri had been in. No answer. I pushed it open slowly. Terri was right where she had been lying on the bed. But she was no longer reading. Her eyes were closed and the book was still open in her hand, resting on the bed.

She was fully clothed but I thought she looked cold. She was lying on top of the duvet. I carefully pulled it out. She moved a bit. I laid the duvet over her but not before I'd taken the book out of her hand.

There was a chair in the corner of the room in front of some enormous wardrobes. I sat down and opened the book. It was called *Oliver Twist* by Charles Dickens. Do you know that one? I didn't.

I still don't, really; it was way too difficult for me. For instance, the first sentence alone had one hundred and one words in it! I know, that's mad, right? One hundred and one. 101. Here's some of the words from the opening sentence: prudent, refrain, fictitious, inasmuch, prefixed. I promise I didn't make any of them up.

I guessed that Terri was really smart. I tried to read on, but before I'd finished a page my own eyes had closed.

As I fell asleep I realised it had only been that morning that I found out about Lil' Legacy and ran to stop Prince. It was just that afternoon that my uncle had decided we were more trouble than we were worth. And it was only a few short hours ago that we'd met Mr Green.

I think that was the longest day of my life.

I slept well.

Chapter 13

With all this talk of trouble, I thought I should tell you about the worst trouble I got into before this began. Before I moved to England. Before my parents sent us away.

My father had got home at the normal time. The back wheel of his bike made a clunking noise every time it turned, so we heard him coming from inside the house. I loved that bike. I dreamed of the day when I could have one just like it. I wanted to ride with my father. But it was too big for me, even to practise on.

My mother went out to meet him, to tell him what my teacher had said. When they came inside he said, 'Come with me, Emmanuel, and bring that.'

We were walking towards the water pump. I was carrying the big water bottle, as my father had told me to. We filled that bottle up a few times a day. It was so big that once it was full I had to roll it; it was too heavy to lift.

I remember feeling sick every step we took on that journey. I had been waiting for hours for my father to get home. I knew he was going to speak to me.

'We are so disappointed with you, Emmanuel,' my father said.

These few words made me well up, a stray tear running down my cheek.

'But he was laughing at Prince, Dadda.' My voice cracked as I tried to defend myself.

'There is never an excuse for fighting, Emmanuel.' Tears were rolling down my face now. 'I don't care what that boy said or did. There is never a reason to fight. Never. Do you understand me, Emmanuel?'

'He made Prince cry and I couldn't. . .'

'Never, Emmanuel.' My father said this so firmly, my mouth clamped shut on what I was going to say and I tasted the salty tears in my mouth. 'Later, you will tell me exactly what happened and what you could have done differently, but now you will collect water on your own. You will collect the water on your own every day until you have shown Prince a good example. He looks up to you, Emmanuel. If he sees you fighting, he will fight. You must show him the right way to behave.'

We did talk later and I collected lots of water. But I still wasn't sure. Is fighting never right?

***

When I woke up, Terri had taken the book back. She was sitting on the bed, reading, and light was streaming through the window. I stretched and she looked up from her book.

'So, you're Emmanuel, right?' She placed her thumb in the book to keep her place as she said this.

'Yep,' I replied, 'and you're Terri.' I felt embarrassed. I'd only just met this girl and I'd fallen asleep in the same room as her. She probably thought I was really weird. I brushed down my creased and blood-stained clothes as she asked me another question.

'What do you think of the book, Emmanuel?'

This seemed like a funny question and I thought about lying, but decided not to. 'I didn't get far, it was a bit hard for me.'

'Do you like books?' she asked. She put the book down on the bed next to her, quickly checking what page she was on while I thought about my answer.

'Some. Do you?' I replied.

Her face lit up. 'Yeah. I love books. This one's OK,' she said, holding up the book she'd been reading, 'but mostly I like mysteries. Have you read any Agatha Christie books?' I could honestly say that I had never heard of Agatha Christie. In fact, I'd never even heard the name Agatha before.

I opened my mouth to answer but at that moment there was a shout from downstairs that sounded like Jamal.

'Come on, you lot, get a move on. We've gotta go in ten minutes.'

Terri jumped up. 'Mr Green must be here.' She looked at me still sitting there. She gave me a questioning look as if to ask 'What are you doing?' but instead said, 'Come on!' Maybe she was scared of Mr Green.

We all met downstairs in the living room. Mr Green was waiting for us, and Jamal was herding everyone through the door. Mr Green told us that it was time to go, and all the others seemed to understand. They gathered their scant belongings, which were similar to mine and Prince's, a few clothes and a few personal items bundled into old bags.

We left the house in pairs or threes, each group waiting for a minute till the other had gone. I left with Prince, who was grinning. Maybe it felt like a game to him. We all met on the corner. Mr Green told us to walk in pairs like we'd done on school trips. That's called a walking bus, I think.

Prince was still smiling as we set off. 'Where are we going, Em?' he asked.

I had no idea. Jamal was walking in front of us, next to Ibby, so I leaned forward to ask him. 'Where are we going?'

Jamal turned round with a grin. 'We're going to work.' Jamal's grin was infectious. Me and Prince turned to each other, grinning. We both remembered what Mr Green had promised to teach us. He seemed like a magician. Making that wallet disappear and reappear.

Jamal craned to look over the heads of the few children in front of him; checking that Mr Green was engrossed in a phone conversation.

He then dropped back beside me. 'Mr Green picks somewhere for us to work,' he said. 'Could be in town, a train station, anywhere really.

We go to work for the day and then later on Mr Green will take us to a new empty house. We'll stay at that house for a week, maybe two, then Mr Green finds us another one.'

It didn't seem like much of an explanation. I had lots of questions to ask, but as Jamal finished, Mr Green called out, 'Jamal, get over here.'

Jamal went jogging off to the front of the line straight away.

I've asked myself many times why Mr Green was allowed to walk fourteen children around a city in broad daylight. But what would you do if you saw fourteen children walking in a line behind an adult? Think school trip? I'm sure you'd never guess the truth. Mr Green wasn't stupid.

Prince walked on and started chatting to Ibby. I stared straight ahead, lost in thought until I felt a tap on my shoulder. I looked around to dark eyes.

'So, Agatha Christie?'

I smiled a broad smile at Terri, but she just looked at me, waiting for me to answer.

'I've never heard of that person,' I told her, and Terri's mouth dropped open.

'You've never heard of Agatha Christie?' She looked a bit stunned but also like she was joking.

'She's the best!'

I shook my head to confirm that I definitely hadn't heard of her.

'So what are these 'some books' that you do like?' she asked.

I had to think hard. I really wasn't a big reader. My class teacher in Year Six had read us *Prince Caspian* and *The Horse and his Boy* from the Chronicles of Narnia.

'Do you like the Narnia books?' I asked.

Terri's face lit up again - her big brown eyes got even bigger. 'Which is your favourite?' she said.

But before I could answer Jamal had rejoined us. When I looked round, Terri seemed to have disappeared.

'Right,' Jamal began, 'Prince, you're with me today. Emmanuel, Kieran's gonna look after you. Kieran's OK,' he said loudly, almost shouting, 'as long as he doesn't try to pinch any purses!'

Ibby burst into laughter and Kieran shouted from a few places forward. 'Shut up! That lady was well strong.'

Ibby turned round, still smirking. 'Kieran got beaten up by an old lady last week. It was well funny.'

Prince was giggling. I wasn't.

I think it was then that it sunk in, what we were going to be doing. I knew I'd stolen that wallet, but that had been once, to survive. This was something different. This was organised. I don't know why that made a difference but it did. We were going to be stealing from people and it was all planned.

Jamal fell back into conversation with Prince and Ibby, and before long they were all laughing. I looked back to find Terri. She was right at the back of the line, her head down. I walked the rest of the way deep in thought.

Chapter 14

I was practised at being silent. I had spent many hours of lessons trying to be invisible. Silence was important to me.

There was a group of boys at my primary school who began to notice me. They even made up a game with me. They would try their hardest to make me break my silence. They were trying to get me noticed. It was horrible.

One lesson we were being taught about how other children in the world lived.

'In some parts of the world,' the teacher was saying from the front, 'children have to go to work at the age of five.'

One of the group of boys sat next to me at my table. As the teacher turned to click to the next slide on the board, he poked me. Not hard but right in the ribs.

I didn't react but looked up at the slide. It was a picture of a boy and girl with bare feet carrying a load of rocks on their backs.

He poked me again.

'Why do you think these children have to work?' The teacher said and a few hands went up. The teacher picked a girl.

'Because they're slaves, Miss?'

'Some of them might be, Shelley. Good idea. Why else might they have to work?' The teacher then picked a boy across the other side of the classroom.

'Because they're really poor, Miss.'

The boy next to me poked me again and I could hear his friends sniggering.

'Is being poor funny to you, Ali?' The teacher addressed one of the boys from the group.

'Sorry, miss,' Ali said.

The teacher continued, addressing the boy who had answered. 'You're right, they're very poor, they can only just afford enough food to survive.' Another poke. 'They don't get new clothes.' Poke. 'Or computer games.' The teacher looked around at some of the boys as another poke hit the same spot. 'Or make-up.' She looked at some of the girls. Another poke. She turned round to show another picture. Poke, poke, poke.

I still didn't react.

The next picture was a group of children standing in front of a little building. The building looked like the first pig's house. You know, made of straw.

'Some of these children,' the teacher continued, 'have to look after their whole family.'

One boy shouted out, smiling, 'What, no adults, Miss?'

Everyone laughed while I received another poke.

The teacher smiled along with the class, then said, 'That might sound like fun for a while but imagine the responsibility of looking after your family, no mum and dad to look after you. Imagine you had to do that.'

One more poke and I exploded.

I screamed in rage, threw my chair backwards and leapt on the boy. 'Stop it, stop it, stop it!' I shouted at him. I was so angry.

This was one of the times that my school did try to call home. They got no answer. The boy admitted that he had been poking me. I didn't get in too much trouble. The teacher kept us in at lunchtime. We both had to say sorry.

I remember feeling angry and shaky for hours. I don't know why. They had tried poking me before.

Chapter 15

Mr Green took us all to a really wide, long road. Both sides were lined with shops. It was as if I'd been shrunk to half my size, then put in a normal-sized high street, it was that big.

We took the bus to get there. Again, I guess the bus driver assumed we were on a school trip. We took up most of the top deck. Jamal and his friends spread across twice as many seats as they needed. Prince sat with me for some of the journey, then Jamal called him over.

It was a sunny day. A day for being outside.

When we got off the bus Kieran approached me. 'So, have you done this before?' he said.

'What?'

'You know, stolen stuff, picked pockets, thieved things?'

'Erm, not really. I've stolen a few things. But I've not done *this*,' I replied.

He didn't look worried at my lack of experience. He smiled at me, a wicked grin. 'No problem, it gets easy. You can just watch me for a while if you like. Be a look-out and that.'

'OK,' I said. Being a look-out did sound easy, but something was worrying me. 'Is it dangerous?' I blurted out. 'Could we get caught?' My uncle's face flashed before my eyes. Standing over me, holding out the last wedge of money he'd given us. 'I don't want to get caught,' I finished.

Kieran looked thoughtful for a moment. Then he said, 'It can be dangerous, if you act like an idiot. You see Ibby?' He nodded towards his friend. Ibby was in a revolving door of a posh-looking shop. A security guard was telling him to stop but he was still going round and round, laughing the whole time.

I smiled at Kieran and said, 'Yeah.'

'Well, Ibby sometimes acts like an idiot. A few months ago he tried to nick this guy's laptop. The guy was working on it at the time. The guy tripped him and held him down. You know how he got away?'

I shook my head.

Kieran answered his question with two words. 'Mr Green. Like I say, it can be dangerous, but you make money for Mr Green and he'll look after you.'

I looked over at Mr Green, who had been on the phone all this time. All the kids had scattered between the bus stop and the shop fronts. Mr Green still seemed pretty great, but I couldn't help but wonder what he did to the guy with the laptop. As I was looking at him, Mr Green hung up his phone and started gathering us all by the bus-stop. When we were together he looked around. I guess he was making sure that no passers-by were too close.

'Right, you lot, listen up.' We pressed in closer. 'Same rewards as normal, best steals mean first in the new house and first pick of the food. Listen to each other and keep your eyes open. Back here at three o'clock. And people,' he said with a grin, 'have fun.'

Most of the others started to disappear. Carla and Sofina went off, giggling. Dwayne, Michael and Ibby sloped off in a little knot. I looked for Terri but couldn't see her anywhere.

Mr Green had one more thing to say. 'Jamal, Kieran, you look after these two, all right?'

Jamal answered him. 'Of course. We'll make them into proper little thieves by the end of the day.'

Somehow, Jamal's words were comforting, and we parted from Mr Green, grinning. In spite of my earlier worries about stealing from people, I couldn't help but be excited. We were learning to be thieves. It was like a TV programme.

I enjoyed watching Kieran work on that first day. We'd wander until he found a likely target, someone too busy to notice or too slow to stop him. He took all sorts of stuff, phones, wallets, a passport. Sometime in the middle of the morning he pinched some chocolate bars for us.

We had agreed to meet Jamal and Prince at one o'clock for lunch. It was nearly time, when Kieran said, 'Right, now it's your turn.'

'What?' I said.

'Come on, it's time to step up. You'll be fine.'

We spent five minutes looking out for an easy target for me. Kieran spotted a lady with a back-pack, a side pocket unzipped.

'Just dip your hand in,' he said, 'and see what you get. Lucky dips are sometimes the best.' He grinned at me.

My heart was already racing.

I dropped into the flow of people walking along the high street and quickly caught up with the lady. I kept with her step for step for about a minute. Suddenly I knew I had to do it right then or I would never do it. My hand darted into her bag, like it had darted across the table and taken a wallet, like it had darted out and picked up some chicken from a barbecue. Into the bag and out; grasping something hard and smooth.

I didn't look at the object, but thrust it into my pocket. I turned and walked towards Kieran, who was watching and waiting. He was smiling at me. I gave him a thumbs-up sign. His smile got even bigger.

When I was a few steps away from him he said, 'What have you got then?'

I pulled the object out of my pocket and found myself proudly holding a brown hair-brush. Kieran burst into laughter, then imitated my thumbs-up sign. I started laughing too. My first 'real' steal was a hair-brush.

'Come on, let's get some lunch,' Kieran said.

Strangely, we didn't steal our lunch. We paid for it out of the money from stolen wallets. Jamal said it was because we couldn't work over our lunch breaks. I guess that made sense.

Prince's morning had been much more successful than mine. He had picked a wallet and a phone. He was beaming with pride. Jamal sang his praises as he told us about the two steals. Kieran clapped him on the back to congratulate him.

We all laughed over my hair-brush.

That afternoon I pinched two phones and the tips that had been left on a restaurant table. At the back of my mind it still felt wrong, taking other people's things.

***

Father used to tell us what was right and what was wrong, and not just when we got into trouble. Usually when we were out, walking or running, Father would stop to look at something and talk to us about it. If we saw someone wasting water, or litter on the ground or even just a plane in the sky, we'd stop and my father would tell us the right and wrong of it.

I remember one day when we had gone into town. Prince was little and had stayed at home with our mother, so it was just me and Father.

The market was busy. Some people were selling and buying but most people were chatting and laughing. We kept stopping. Lots of the men wanted to talk to my father. They asked him questions and he usually made a joke. They would clap each other on the shoulders and laugh, then say goodbye and we would walk on, trying to find the items my mother had sent us to buy.

We found the first item, a ball of string at a market stall covered in useful-looking things. Scissors, rope, hammers. Some things were worn and old-looking, others new, like the scissors that glinted in the sun. I moved my head back and forth so the gleam of light shone in and out of my eyes as my father talked about the price of the string. It took a long time.

When we walked on, the string in my hand, I asked my father, 'Why did you have to talk about the price, Dadda?'

My father scratched his nose and replied, 'You see all these things, Emmanuel?' He stretched out his arms to take in the whole market.

I nodded and said, 'Yes, Dadda.'

'All these things have a price, Emmanuel, they are all worth something.'

I nodded.

'Sometimes we don't want to pay the price, we think they are worth less than the price. You understand?'

I nodded again.

'And sometimes we can't pay as much as the price. So we have to talk, we have to come to an agreement.' My father finished there but I had another question.

'What if you can't pay the price, Dadda, and you can't come to an agreement? What do you do then?' I said.

'Then you must walk away empty-handed and maybe work a little harder. Everything has a price and we must work to meet that price. You have to work hard, Emmanuel, then you can have all the best things you can think of. If you don't work hard, then you must go empty-handed. That is why you must carry all the things we buy - and then I will give you a sweet.' My father laughed. 'That is the price,' he said. 'Do you agree?' He offered his hand to me.

'What if I carry half of the things?' I replied with a smile, and offered my hand in return.

He grabbed my hand and pulled me towards him. He kissed me on the top of the head and said, 'It's a deal.'

***

So it really felt wrong taking other people's things. But even so, there was something fun about it.

It starts with a slightly sick feeling as you look for your target. That's the worst bit. Then as soon as you've decided who to go for, your heart starts beating so hard and the sick feeling turns into butterflies. The beating and the butterflies get stronger and faster as you approach the target. Then comes the moment when you know you've got to act and you think your heart is going to burst out of your chest. Then your hand moves and the moment is gone and you feel like you've scored the best goal ever.

Yeah, robbing stuff had an upside.

At the end of the day, we all met by the bus stop we'd started from. Each person handed over to Mr Green what they'd taken. I don't know if some of the kids kept stuff back for themselves, but I handed everything over, even the hair-brush.

Mr Green held it up and smiled at me. 'Lucky dip?' he asked.

I nodded.

'Well done, Emmanuel,' he said, when I gave him the mobile phones and the loose change.

He made a big fuss of Prince's haul. By the end of the day Prince had stolen two phones, like me, three wallets, a watch and a laptop.

'Wow!' Mr Green said. 'That's some good work, Prince. He's nearly as good as you, Jamal.'

Jamal was standing next to Prince, his arm round his shoulders. 'I don't know about that, Mr Green, but he is good. He took that pretty much right out of someone's hand,' he said, pointing at the gold-coloured watch.

'OK,' Mr Green said loudly, 'I want to talk to you two.' He pointed at Freddie and Sastre.

The whole group was silent, and the two boys who had been singled out went white.

'Apart from that, well done,' Mr Green called out, and there were sighs of relief that no one else was in the same position as Freddie and Sastre. 'I think we have our winners for the day. First picks at the new house go to Jamal and 'lightning fingers' Prince.'

There were a few cheers and some groans.

Prince was really making a name for himself.

Chapter 16

Prince had learnt to fit in quickly. When we arrived in England, so much changed. We went from parents to an absent uncle. From a home to a house that we feared, but clung to as our little shred of security. From being looked after to looking after ourselves.

It was cold when we arrived. Compared to the blistering heat of our home village, where the sun beat down on the top of your head and the ground blistered your feet, a windy English summer is so cold. We got off the plane into a vast airport, but I don't remember much except the cold.

We were asked questions about who we were travelling with and why our parents weren't with us.

Prince remained silent and I explained that we were visiting our uncle. My parents had put in place the pretence of a visit to see my uncle, and I kept it up for Prince's sake.

I told them that my uncle would be waiting for us in the airport. I showed them his phone number and address. That seemed OK with them.

As soon as we found a phone I used the telephone number that my parents had given us. My uncle was not surprised to hear from us. My father had written to him weeks before. He told us how to find him.

Dazed, we wandered through the airport. So many new sights: vast shops, enormous television screens and people of so many different, pale colours.

We soon got used to all these things. We were both good at adjusting, but Prince was better at fitting in.

***

By the second night with Mr Green's gang, Prince had fitted right in. It was probably then that they started calling him 'Flash'. Jamal, Ibby, Kieran and Flash. In no time at all Prince was shining like he always did. That first day was not the only time that he was the best thief of the day. Suddenly, he was right at the centre of the gang, while I found myself on the edge.

If there had been a list of who was in charge of the gang, after Mr Green, Jamal would have been at the top, with his friends just behind. Me and Terri would have been at the bottom.

It wasn't that I did anything wrong. I got on with everybody, I stole things as well as I could and I was nice to the right people. I think I was right at the bottom for three reasons. One, because stealing never came naturally to me like it did to Prince. Two, because Jamal took a dislike to me. And three, because I was friends with Terri.

We continued our conversation about books on that second evening in the new, empty house that Mr Green had taken us to.

I found Terri beside me, with a whisper in my ear. 'Follow me.' She took hold of my hand with two fingers and her thumb - her little, white hands pinching my dark skin. She led me out of the back door, to a bench at the bottom of the new house's garden. None of the neighbours could see into this garden, so Mr Green had said that we could use it.

'So, your favourite Narnia book?'

I had forgotten where our earlier conversation had stopped and I had to think back carefully.

'Erm, *The Horse and his Boy*, I think,' I replied.

'Oh, that's a good choice. I like *The Last Battle*.'

For all the time I knew her, me and Terri's conversations were often like that. She would start from wherever we'd been interrupted earlier in the day, or where we'd fallen asleep the night before. Her memory was amazing. She never forgot what we'd been talking about.

Terri's favourite things to talk about were books and stories, but we talked about other stuff too.

'I found this in the house,' Terri said, holding up a book with a picture of a pig's head on it. It was called *Lord of the Flies*. 'Have you read this?'

I took it off her and stared at the cover. It looked a bit scary. I had not read it and told Terri so.

'Shall we read it?' she asked. 'I'll read some to you and then you can read to me. OK?'

'OK.' I smiled at her.

Terri read well. Her quiet voice made the characters come alive. She never stuttered or stumbled over words. I didn't do as good a job as her, but she didn't mind. She said that she loved listening as much as she loved reading. Maybe there had been someone who had read to her before.

I never found that out though. Somehow, in all

our hours reading and talking, me and Terri hardly ever talked about our families. We avoided the subject of our pasts, except to tell little stories about school and friends.

She told me about her best friend, Manon. She told me more about Manon's house and home than her own.

Manon and Terri were writing a story together. It was for a school project but they carried it on after the project was finished. Terri did most of the writing and Manon did the pictures. Terri called the pictures illustrations.

The story was about two friends who went to boarding school together. Terri told me it was like *Mallory Towers*, but I'd never heard of that.

They used to do all of it at Manon's house. When I asked why they couldn't do it at Terri's house, she mumbled something about her dad and then quickly changed the subject.

A few weeks later, following days and days of playing the part of thieves and two more moves into new, empty houses, me and Terri finished *Lord of the Flies*. We decided that we didn't really like it. It scared us, but we still finished it.

As Terri closed the book for the last time she

asked me, 'Do you think our lives will change?'

'What?' I replied. I didn't know what she meant.

'Do you think we'll always be with Mr Green?'

'Erm, I don't know. I guess not.' I hadn't thought about this. I was happy not to be in charge. I was happy that someone else was looking after Prince. I was happy to be away from my uncle and his friends. There weren't many things that I'd been happy about before Mr Green found us. 'Do you want things to be different?' I asked.

'I don't know, I think I want a proper home, Em. Don't you?'

A proper home? For the first time in a long time I almost shed a tear. I thought about my mother and father. I remembered when Prince used to really smile. I could see our old home and smell the dust in the air.

'I guess I do,' I replied.

Me and Terri were both lost in thought after this exchange. But we returned to the subject many times over the following weeks.

A proper home.

Chapter 17

I guess there are some things you are wondering about. Here's one thing I think you would like to know the answer to. How did Mr Green always find empty homes to house the gang? I didn't find out the answer to this till much later.

Mr Green had a friend who worked for an airline. I think it was one of those really cheap ones. You know, the 'fly somewhere for £5' ones. Mr Green's friend did something with computers for them. He was able to go into all the files on their computers.

Mr Green paid him money each time that he found what Mr Green needed. A big family, who were going on holiday, leaving an empty house. Mr Green would make a phone call, his friend would go on his computer, and as if by magic we had a house to sleep in.

Here's something else you might be wondering about. Didn't the neighbours ever notice? I guess a lot of the neighbours weren't that bothered about what went on next door. But sometimes they were. Sometimes we got into trouble. Once we nearly got caught.

We were staying in this massive house. It was in the south half of the city, over the river. It was full of loads of interesting stuff. Including thousands of books.

We had been there for a few hours. Jamal and his friends had found some stuffed animals and were charging round the house with them. Julia and her friends were playing in the enormous garden. Carla and Sofina were upstairs trying on the clothes that the house's owners had left behind. Terri was rooting through the book shelves, trying to find something she'd like to read. I was sitting close by, watching my brother.

Prince had a stuffed fox's head. He was holding it up in front of his face and doing silly voices. Ibby was giggling. I was smiling too.

Prince smiled over at me. 'Hey, Em, do your impression of an old man,' he shouted.

But before I could respond we heard a sound that made us freeze. Police sirens. Lots of police sirens, getting nearer.

Carla and Sofina came charging down the stairs and Carla shouted, 'They're coming this way!'

By the time the pair had reached the bottom of the stairs we were all heading for the door. We pushed each other out of the way. Terri was left at the back.

I grabbed Prince's hand and ran. Through the kitchen. Out the back door. Across the garden. Over a back fence. Another garden. Down an alleyway at the side of a house. Following the person in front. Being followed by others.

That was terrifying. Not knowing whether it was a policeman you could hear two steps behind, or a friend. I held on to Prince the whole time we ran. We stopped a few streets away, in front of a closed newsagent, and I finally let go of his wrist as he shook me off with a tut.

'You didn't need to drag me.' I looked at him. He looked back at me angrily, then glanced over at Jamal. Jamal was leaning against the wall, staring at us.

'Whoa!' Ibby screamed, his face to the sky. 'We made it.'

Everyone else was still catching their breath. I watched Jamal straighten up and then look around. 'Everyone all right?' he panted.

People gave nods or breathed out a yes. I looked around, scanning the faces. Julia, Kammy, Dwayne, Kieran, Carla supporting Sofina, Alex, Sastre, Ibby, Freddie, Jamal, Prince. Where was Terri?

I thought this and then said it out loud. 'Where's Terri?'

Jamal looked around too, and then echoed my question. 'Where is Terri?'

Everyone was looking round now. Terri definitely wasn't there.

Jamal looked down the street we'd come from, then said, 'Mr Green is gonna be well pissed if she's been arrested.' Prince was looking at me. A worried expression crossed his face. 'She's such an idiot. He's gonna kill us!' Jamal continued.

'Are we going back for her?' I said.

Ibby snorted a laugh but it was Jamal who replied. 'Are you mad? Go back for *her* and get ourselves arrested too?'

I glanced round the group. I couldn't believe they

would all agree with Jamal, but no one spoke up.

'I've gotta call Mr Green. Where's a phone box?' Jamal said. Jamal was the only one in the group who had Mr Green's phone number.

'You're serious?' I said. 'We're not even going back to look for her?' I could feel myself beginning to get angry. The kind of anger where you can't stop yourself exploding. Even if you're speaking to someone that you know you should be nice to.

Jamal stared at me. He wasn't used to people questioning him.

'Shut up, Em,' Kieran said, taking hold of my arm lightly.

'But she could be in trouble!' I said, brushing Kieran off and staring back at Jamal. I could feel most of the group backing away. Out of the corner of my eye I could see Prince, his gaze shared between me and Jamal.

'Emmanuel, shut up.' This time it was Prince who spoke.

But before I could answer, Jamal spat, 'You're a fool, Emmanuel! I mean it, Mr Green is gonna be so pissed. But don't worry, I'll just tell him that it was your fault she got caught. Maybe he won't take it out on the rest of us then.'

I carried on staring at Jamal. I was seconds away from exploding. Then I heard a shout.

'There she is!' I turned round to see Terri trotting along the road towards us. She was almost smiling.

I looked at Prince. He gave a big sigh of relief. Maybe he was relieved because Terri was safe, maybe because of what I might have done if she hadn't turned up, but I think it was because he didn't want to see an angry Mr Green. Prince had seen enough angry adults.

***

When we first saw my uncle in England he was angry. He came out to the airport to get us. He didn't hug us like he used to or even smile. Prince clung on to my hand. I clung on to Prince's too.

We got a train from the airport into town. My uncle didn't speak to us much. He asked a few questions about our journey but he mostly stared out of the window.

Then I remembered what my mother had told me. 'My dadda says you were right, Uncle Victor.' I spoke quietly, looking at the uncle who felt like a stranger.

Uncle Victor took his gaze from the window and fixed it on me. 'It makes no difference,' he said. 'He is there in trouble and I am here in trouble.' Then he resumed staring out of the window.

When we arrived at my uncle's house there were several men and women there. They were all as dark as my uncle and all looked as displeased to see us as he had.

One woman shouted, 'What are they doing here, Victor?'

'What am I supposed to do with them?' my uncle shouted back.

'I don't care, just get them out of here!' The woman stormed out of the room and my uncle followed.

We were left with strangers. Some stared at us, others carried on with what they had been doing before we disturbed them. Two men were playing cards whilst smoking long cigarettes, another was picking at some food.

A woman who had been sitting on the lap of one of the card players got up and came over. 'Don't you worry, just go and sit yourselves down.' She pointed us through to another room. We went and sat down.

We stayed in that room all night. We didn't know where my uncle had gone. Prince cried a lot. I didn't.

I've never really been one for crying.

In the morning my uncle took us to the house with the plants. We never saw where he lived again.

Chapter 18

I used to love playing football with Prince. I mean just me and him. Before we met Jamal and everyone else, me and Prince were best friends. I guess he was my only real friend. He was the only person who knew all about me.

Just me and Prince with a football, in a park or in our garden, before it got too overgrown. We didn't even need goal-posts or anything. We just ran around chasing the ball, trying to tackle each other.

Prince was much better than me, he could do all sorts of skills. He would watch different players and try to copy them, or watch the older kids at school. He was much more skilful but

I was stronger, so it was quite an even match.

I remember sunny days, days when most people would call it hot, playing in the park. A big open space in front of us. We could run and laugh and shout as much as we wanted. We didn't need to be quiet or to be invisible. No one was watching us there. After a while I didn't even notice anyone else. Just the ball and my brother.

'Watch this!' Prince would pant. Then he'd attempt some new trick that he'd learnt. Trying to thread the ball through my legs or through his own. Sometimes he'd get past me, laughing or shouting, 'Come and get me, slow-coach!' Sometimes I'd force him off the ball and I'd be the one laughing.

It reminded me of home. Of running and laughing and playing with my father. Me and Prince and Dadda. Mum would often watch us running around outside. She would clap her hands together and call encouragement. 'Go on, Emmy!' or 'Keep chasing, my little Prince!'

Me and Prince were best friends then. But we weren't best friends any more, after we joined the gang. We went our separate ways, Prince with Jamal and Ibby and Kieran, and me with Terri.

Prince was 'one of the boys'. When we were

working, he usually worked with Jamal or Ibby, or sometimes Kieran. I thought I might write, 'they were thick as thieves', but they *were* thieves, so I couldn't really.

That's not to say that me and Prince stopped being close. Well, not straight away. He was still my brother. So sometimes I would do my stealing with Prince, or with Prince and his friends. Other days I would work with Terri or Kammy or Sastre.

I liked working with Prince or Terri the best. It was usually really fun with Prince. We laughed and played and it felt, well, it felt like we were brothers. Although along with the fun it was scary. As the days went by and Prince became more and more adapted to the gang life, he became more and more angry. Angry like my uncle. Sometimes when we were working, he'd screw his face up and he'd even look like my uncle. Then I knew someone could get hurt.

A few weeks after we started stealing, I worked with Prince for the last time. He had stolen loads, as usual. He didn't stop, but almost ran from one steal to the next.

'Come on, Em,' he hissed when I slowed him down. I had only stopped to tie my shoe-lace.

We had lunch with Jamal and his friends. Prince

always did, and when I was working with Prince I had to as well. We had burgers and chips, which made me think of our first day in London. I remembered a terrified, silent Prince, but he was long gone.

As we were eating, an old man came over to us. He looked different from anyone I'd ever seen. He wore a spotty piece of material round his neck which billowed out of his shirt. He also had a wooden walking stick and a hat made of straw, perched on his head.

'So why aren't you lot in school then?' he asked. His face was so wrinkled, I couldn't tell whether he was kind or angry.

Jamal was the first to reply. He said, 'What the hell does it have to do with you?'

'Pardon me, young man, but is that any way to talk to your elder?' the old man replied, and I couldn't help but agree.

'My what? Someone do something about this guy,' Jamal said.

Just then Prince stood up. His face was a mask of anger and I was taken back to that day when we had left my uncle.

'Get out of here!' Prince shouted, kicking out at the old man's cane.

I leapt out of my seat and grabbed both my brother's arms. 'Prince!' I said.

He rounded on me, shaking his arms free. 'Get the hell off me!' he shouted. For a moment I thought he was going to hit me. I continued to stare at my brother, but he didn't look like him. Then Jamal laughed, Ibby laughed, Kieran laughed and eventually Prince laughed.

I didn't. I finished that lunch in silence.

It was not the same with Terri. We only did a bit of pick-pocketing because we had to. Mostly we just sat or walked or found a library or bookshop. We talked a lot. Terri loved reading and talking. She hated stealing. But like all of us, she needed safety and Mr Green kept us safe.

The one time she did talk about her home it didn't sound safe.

I had asked her what her mum and dad were like.

She didn't say anything for a long time and I thought she must be really upset. Then she said quietly, 'Mum wasn't around.'

I didn't know what to say to that, so I didn't say anything.

'I tried to stay away from my dad as much as possible,' she said. 'If I did go near him I had to do exactly as he said. Exactly as he said, Emmanuel.'

I think I knew what she meant. Like I said, it didn't sound safe.

Chapter 19

If I had given titles to my chapters, the title to this one would be *The Return of the Wallet Man*. Or it could be *How Stupid does Emmanuel Get?* Or maybe *Forgiveness*.

I only worked with Jamal once. He told me that he wanted to see how I was getting on, so he was gonna work with me the next day. I was pretty nervous. I knew I really wasn't very good at stealing stuff, but I didn't want Mr Green to know. I didn't know what would happen if Mr Green decided that he wanted 'to talk to me'.

I hadn't asked Freddie and Sastre what had happened to them when Mr Green had 'talked' to them. But they had seemed different the next day, quieter, and Freddie had a cut over his right eye.

I woke up nervous. The sun was peeking in between the curtains. Me and Prince were sharing a room, and he woke up as I stirred.

'I'm working with Jamal today,' I told him.

'Cool,' Prince said, yawning.

'Do you think he likes me?'

'What? I don't know.' He stifled another yawn and stretched, the duvet cover dropping down his t-shirt as he sat up. 'Jamal's cool, you don't need to worry,' he said.

I was still worried, but I wasn't sure why.

Mr Green took us to work in all sorts of places, high streets, big train stations, shopping centres. But that day we were at an airport. Just like a train station, but bigger and busier - and a lot more stuff to steal.

When we arrived and Mr Green had talked to us all, Jamal put his arm round me and said, 'Come on then, Emmy, let's see what you've got!'

That didn't help my nerves.

We started out small. We took a few purses that people had left by the sides of chairs as they waited. Jamal lifted a phone from someone's pocket. I got close to taking a wallet out of a man's open bag. But I wasn't fast enough though.

I edged towards him slowly, through the crowd. I could see the leather just peeking out of an open pocket. The man with the bag was standing still, looking up at a screen that showed when planes were leaving.

I took my time because I was still a bit nervous and shaky. Jamal was watching me carefully. I didn't know what he was looking for, but I thought maybe he was looking to see me make a mistake. So, slowly, slowly I went.

Just as I was about to dip my hand in and make the final move, the man swore and then set off running. Maybe he was missing his plane.

'What the hell was that?' Jamal asked when I returned to where he was watching.

'What?'

'What were you doing?'

'I was just a bit slow,' I replied.

I could tell he was not impressed. 'A bit slow?' he said. 'That was more than 'a bit slow', that was rubbish. I thought you might be good at this, I can't believe Flash is your brother. Come on.'

Jamal turned and walked away.

I felt sick. I was angry with Jamal. I didn't want him to tell Mr Green or Prince about what had just happened but I felt he would be telling everyone.

I was right. Over lunch he replayed the whole incident to Ibby, Kieran, Dwayne, Michael and Prince.

They all laughed at me. Kieran said, 'You're almost as spazzy as Ibby.' Ibby punched him on the arm.

That made me feel a bit better. They did laugh at each other as well as me. But Jamal's looks of disdain were only for me. I was determined that I was going to prove him wrong in the afternoon.

Again, we started out slow. Just a few easy steals. But all the time I was looking out for something good. A steal that would impress Jamal.

About an hour after lunch I saw it. A man in a smart suit carrying a briefcase and a laptop bag. That was bound to be worth a lot of credit. I pointed him out to Jamal and we followed the man for a while, looking for an opportunity.

It came when he bent down to tie his shoe-lace. He put both his bags down beside him. I was going to take both of them. There was probably good stuff in the briefcase, I thought.

He was about twenty metres away from us and I

knew I needed to be quick. I set off at a sprint, dodging past a family. They were pulling large suitcases and I nearly tripped over one.

Seconds later I was slowing down and crouching, ready to snatch the bags. I was a metre away when the man started to straighten up. Our hands reached the handles of the bags at the same time. I gripped on tightly and so did he. We both went tumbling to the ground.

I was on my feet straight away, still clinging to the bag. He was not as quick getting up, but he was much stronger. I was going nowhere.

I took my eyes off the bags and looked at the man just as he looked at me. I knew that face. Then I remembered.

'SD,' I said before I could stop myself.

'What? It's you!' the man said. 'So I didn't just lose my wallet!'

I didn't know what to say or do. I just stood there.

He had stood up by now, but we both still clung to the bags.

'Do you do this for a living?' he said. 'Do you?'

I didn't reply.

'Do you need help?'

I carried on staring at him. Maybe I nodded.

'I'm not bothered about the wallet, I'm not going to call the police. Don't worry.'

I still just stood there, staring, so he carried on speaking.

'Maybe I can help you. Take this,' he said. He let go of his briefcase slowly, and with his free hand he reached into his jacket pocket and pulled out a leaflet. He held it out to me. I had both my hands on the handles of his bags, but I was curious. How did he think this piece of paper could help me?

I let go of the briefcase and it dropped to the floor. I reached out towards the leaflet. As my hand closed around it, the man collapsed to the floor. Jamal was standing behind him and he shouted, 'Run!'

Jamal must have kicked the back of his legs, but I didn't wait around to find out. I ran and Jamal followed. The man had held on to his laptop, but I had the leaflet screwed up in my fist. I shoved the piece of paper into my pocket as I ran.

We ran hard, in and out of the crowd. No one tried to get in our way. We stopped behind a kiosk selling scarves and ties. Jamal looked back. No one was following.

Before I got my breath back, Jamal slapped me across the face.

'You fool!' He said. 'Why the hell didn't you run? Did you think you were going to pull the bag out of his hand?'

I thought about hitting Jamal back. I thought about answering him. I even thought about running away from him. But I knew that there was nothing I could do or say. Jamal was right. Why didn't I run?

I stuck to simple steals for the rest of the day. Jamal barely spoke to me, but once we met up with the others, he wouldn't stop talking. He told everyone about my mistakes. 'What a fool!' he said.

Prince laughed as hard as everyone else, and clung to Jamal and his friends.

***

That evening, back at the house we were staying in, Terri tried to talk to me.

'Don't worry,' she said. 'Jamal's an idiot.'

'I'm not worried,' I replied, not looking at her, and staring at a book that I wasn't reading.

'Just don't let him get to you, Em.' She put her nose back in her book and we continued in silence.

A while later, maybe ten minutes, maybe half an hour, I was still not reading.

Terri looked up again. 'What is it, Em? What's the matter?'

I looked at her then. 'I don't want to do this,' I replied. 'I don't want to stay with Mr Green and Jamal. I don't want to steal things.'

'Me neither.' She said this really quietly, as if she didn't want anyone to hear.

'OK, we won't. We'll find somewhere else to go.' I knew that it was not so simple, but in that moment I wished that it could be.

'OK,' she said again quietly, and this time sadly. She knew as well as I did that we could wish all we liked, but we had nowhere else to go and no one else to help us.

From that day I was determined. We weren't staying with Mr Green. Me and Terri and, I hoped, Prince. 'There must be someone who will help us, someone better.'

I just didn't know who.

Chapter 20

I was desperate to get away from Mr Green for many reasons, but one day all these reasons got overtaken by another. On that day Mr Green was no longer the magic thief who could make wallets disappear and reappear. That day I knew, as I hadn't known before, that Mr Green was a real, bad guy.

We were working on a busy high street. The one where I'd spent that first working day with Kieran. Mr Green said it was the best 'money spot'. Lots of tourists. Tourists didn't really watch their bags that carefully.

Me and Terri were looking out for the easiest

steals. Open bags, phones left on tables, loose jackets with big pockets.

I had already taken enough that day and Terri needed to catch up. We were looking for likely targets.

'What about that guy?' Terri said. She pointed to a man with a green backpack. He was passing us on the other side of the road. As Terri pointed, he looked straight at us, and his eyes narrowed. 'Maybe not,' Terri whispered as we disappeared into the crowd.

'What about them?' she said, pointing at a couple of teenage boys who were walking away from us. They both wore caps and I could see why Terri had picked them. One of them had a wallet poking out of the back pocket of his jeans.

'OK,' I replied, 'let's do it.' We strolled through the crowds, slowly catching up with the pair. We could hear them chatting. They had Asian accents and spoke quickly to each other.

When we were a few metres away from them, something happened that made me stop. One of their phones started ringing. It played a tune that I hadn't heard in a long time. The same Lil' Legacy song that my friends, Asad and Ikram, had been singing all that time ago.

I stopped and Terri turned to me.

'Why have you stopped?' she hissed. And then, more gently, 'And what are you smiling for?'

I was smiling. A sad smile. A remembering smile.

***

The rest of the afternoon was much the same. Almost steals and missed steals. Terri didn't take much more and we were worried. Worried that Mr Green might be angry. But in the end Mr Green had something else to be angry about.

We arrived back at the meeting place at the same time as Prince and Kieran. Prince punched me on the arm and said, 'All right, bro!' His mouth was smiling at me but his eyes weren't.

'All right,' I replied and tried to smile back. Terri stood a pace behind me, like she always did when any of Jamal's friends were around, even Prince.

Most of the others were already waiting. Mr Green hadn't arrived yet. Ibby was showing anyone who would look, three watches, all strapped to his wrist. Jamal glared at me for a moment, then beckoned Prince and Kieran over. I saw them begin to compare loot.

'Who are we waiting for?' Terri asked me. 'Apart from Mr Green, I mean.'

We both looked around the group. Most of them were laughing and joking. Carla and Sofina were wearing matching hats today, bright pink. You couldn't miss them.

'Erm,' I began to reply, 'Julia. . .'

'And Sastre,' Terri finished. 'That's not like them, being late.'

'All right you lot, what you got?' Mr Green's voice was clear over the top of everyone's laughter, his London accent strong as usual.

One by the one the kids brought their takings to Mr Green. He inspected, praised, even gave a few winks. It was nearly my turn to approach Mr Green when someone shouted, 'Oi, watch out!' and Julia came crashing into the middle of the group, panting.

'It's Sastre,' she spluttered. 'He's. . . he. . . I think he got caught.'

Ibby was giggling but Mr Green soon stopped him. His large, pale hand swung up and hit Ibby on the back of the head.

'What?' Mr Green exclaimed, not loudly but with real power. 'Where? Show me. Now!'

Julia straightened up and began to lead the way.

'Jamal. Prince.' Mr Green barked and both boys followed. When they were a few paces away, Mr Green called over his shoulder, 'The rest of you wait right there. Stick everything in the bag.'

We knew what he meant by that. Whenever he met us after work he brought a great big, black hold-all. He put all the stolen stuff in it. Me and Terri threw our loot in quickly and waited. Like all the others we waited in near silence. We waited a long time, maybe half an hour, maybe an hour. After a while people started chatting again, but there was no more laughter.

Jamal and Prince returned first. They told us what they knew. 'He was nicking from a shop, the idiot. A fat security guard grabbed 'im,' Jamal said.

'Mr Green'll kill him if he finds him,' Prince chipped in.

A few minutes later Mr Green returned with a sobbing Julia. She was holding one side of her face and there was blood on her swollen lip.

No one spoke. Mr Green picked up the hold-all and we followed him.

As soon as we arrived at another new house Mr Green exploded. He tore open the hold-all and poured the contents on to the floor.

'What is this?' he screamed, kicking a wallet aside. Julia began sobbing again. 'You lazy little. . . !' He looked around at us all. Then, in a lower but equally scary voice, he said, 'How can I look after you if you can't look after yourselves?'

No one answered.

'All of you, keep your heads down. If you cause me any more trouble I'll do more than make you cry.' He said this looking at Julia, then grabbed Jamal by the collar. 'Get in here,' he commanded through gritted teeth. 'You too, Prince.' He beckoned them into the house's large front room.

The others began to disappear, each trying to get as far from Mr Green as possible. I didn't move. What was Mr Green going to do to my brother?

Terri touched me on the arm and whispered, 'Come on, Em.'

I shook my head in reply, then said, 'You go.' I heard her creep off behind me. I had to make sure Prince was OK.

I moved as quietly as I could to the door through which Mr Green had taken Prince and Jamal. When I was a few steps away, I could hear Mr Green's voice clearly.

'What do you mean, there was nothing you could

do?' He was still shouting. 'You are meant to be looking after this bunch of idiots.'

The door was open a crack, so I moved even closer and peered through. Mr Green stood in the middle of the room, towering over Jamal and Prince. They were seated on a sofa. Prince was looking at the floor and I could see that he was close to tears.

Jamal was meeting Mr Green's gaze. He looked defiant. 'What d'you want me to do?' Jamal said. 'Like you say, they're idiots. I can't keep my eye on all of them.'

Mr Green took a step forward and slapped Jamal across the face.

Prince let out a yelp. Jamal looked even angrier but it was Mr Green who spoke first.

'Who do you think you're talking to? I ain't your mate, Jamal!' With that, Mr Green reached inside his jacket pocket and pulled out a gun. He levelled it at Jamal. 'You're gonna watch your tongue, Jamal, and remember who looks after you. Now get out, both of you. I'm staying here tonight.'

For a moment I was rooted to the spot. I couldn't believe what I was seeing. Then I ran.

That evening in the house the gang was different. Less laughter, no games, fewer smiles. All we could talk about was whether Sastre would dob us in.

And all I could think about was whether that would be a bad thing or a good thing.

Chapter 21

Sometimes dreadful things happen and you can do nothing about them. Sometimes you can wish all you like but nothing changes. Sometimes you're powerless. In the end I couldn't change what happened.

It took a surprisingly short time for things to return to normal. A few days, and we were acting like we'd never known a boy called Sastre. A boy who liked football and crisps and had dark, curly hair. We had moved house several times. Mr Green may have been worried. But on the outside he had returned to his normal self too.

A week after I'd seen Mr Green pull a gun on Jamal,

we were staying in a huge house in north London. Big enough for us all to squeeze into and still have room for 'crockery catch'.

Me and Terri were working our way through a new book. I can't remember what it was called, but it was really sad. I do remember the main character's name. He was called William, but people called him Willy. That kept making me laugh. He was a little boy in the war. He got sent to the country and an old man looked after him. Then his friend died and his sister. His mum was horrible too. I don't know what happened at the end. We never got a chance to finish it.

We had been at this house for a few days. We woke up one morning to the sound of Mr Green shouting up the stairs. 'Come on you lot, get up!' He didn't sound happy.

I jumped up from the chair I'd been sleeping on. Terri was lying at the top of the bed, the book open in her hand. Julia, who sometimes liked to hear Terri read, was curled up at the bottom of the bed. I stepped quickly across the room and shook Terri awake.

'What's going on?' I heard Julia murmur through a yawn.

'Mr Green's here,' I replied, and in a moment, Terri and Julia were on their feet, picking up jumpers and books and games and shoving them into bags.

'Come on, we're moving, hurry up!' Mr Green was shouting now and Jamal burst into the room.

'Hurry up,' he growled through gritted teeth.

We grabbed the last of our possessions and flooded down the stairs. It had only taken a few minutes and a bit of fear. All of us were in the hall pulling on shoes and coats.

Mr Green was already at the door, holding it open a crack. He looked really angry. When we were all ready he just said, 'Come on,' and walked out of the door.

Normally we'd have gone a few at a time, as we didn't want the neighbours to get suspicious, but we could see what kind of mood Mr Green was in. I helped Terri put her rucksack on, as me and Prince exchanged looks. He was scared.

I was one of the last through the door, with Terri on my heels. Mr Green was halfway down the street. We ran to catch up. Everyone was hurrying.

Mr Green led us to the same high street where me and Prince had started our life of crime. It wasn't very busy. It was still quite early and most of the people were wearing suits and walking quickly. Not the kind of people you tried to pick-pocket.

We gathered together around Mr Green. He wasn't as confident as usual. He chewed his lip before he spoke.

'Right, you lot, make yourselves scarce. Don't do anything stupid. I want to see you all here at four.' As he said 'here' he pointed to the floor, then motioned with his head and said, 'Jamal.'

Jamal went white as he approached Mr Green. So did Prince, but he stood like a statue.

As the others began to pair off, I walked over to Prince. Terri was waiting for me, but I wanted to talk to my brother.

'Are you OK?' I said.

'Yeah. What?' Prince had become more aggressive over the past few days. He had picked fights with Freddie and Ibby. Nearly all his time was spent with Jamal. I was worried about him but didn't know how to talk to him. How could I tell him I'd been right outside the door and done nothing to help.

'Nothing, it's just,' I lowered my voice, 'Mr Green seems a bit angry.'

'It's fine, don't worry, brother.' And that was it.

Prince still looked anxious but he wasn't going to talk to me about it.

Me and Terri didn't do much stealing that morning. Enough, we hoped. We did not want to be in trouble with Mr Green. After we had done the minimum, we found a nearby park to sit in. We read a bit and talked a lot. We had begun talking more and more about what life could be like without Mr Green.

'You could be a writer,' I told Terri. 'You could carry on the story you started with Manon and write lots of them and be really rich.'

She laughed. 'Only if you would read all of my books and tell me what was rubbish and what was good.'

I agreed to that, it sounded like a fair deal.

Around lunchtime, when we ventured out of the park, we saw Prince and Jamal. They were standing by a fast-food restaurant, laughing as they watched Kieran hold Ibby in a head-lock. Jamal saw us, tapped Prince on the shoulder and pointed us out.

Prince smiled and ran towards us. 'Huh!' Prince faked a punch to my face. I flinched and Prince laughed. I could see Jamal smirking at me, just over Prince's shoulder.

'You were right, Em,' Prince began. 'Mr Green is

really angry. His friend's been arrested. The one that gets us all the houses. That's why we had to move quick this morning. He thinks Sastre must have squealed and told them about the houses.'

I glanced at Terri. She looked worried. I knew that Prince made her nervous but it was more than that.

'Are you sure?' I asked my brother.

'Yeah, Jamal told me,' he replied.

'What are we going to do then, I mean tonight?'

Prince shrugged. 'We'll see later, I guess. In a bit, yeah?' With that he turned and walked back to Jamal.

The rest of the afternoon, Terri and I were both quiet. We talked a little about what Mr Green might do with us. Maybe we'd have to go to his house. Maybe we'd have to just stay outside. Maybe Mr Green would not come back.

I knew that the last idea was why we were both so quiet. We didn't like Mr Green. We wanted to be somewhere, anywhere else, without him. Still, we felt we needed him. Who else would keep us safe?

So we wandered aimlessly until four o'clock came around. Then we joined the others where Mr Green had asked us to meet him. And we waited.

Four fifteen. Four thirty. No Mr Green.

Jamal was keeping everyone occupied. He went round checking what people had stolen that day. He wasn't impressed with me and Terri.

Then, at four thirty-nine, Mr Green showed up. There were a lot of sighs. Maybe everyone was thinking the same thing. However angry Mr Green got, we still needed an adult.

Just like in the morning, he told us, 'Hurry up!' and, 'Come on!' Then he walked and we followed.

We went straight down the high street. Past jewellery shops and shoe shops and souvenir shops, pizza restaurants, burger places and Chinese buffets. Mr Green stopped outside a massive shop. From where we stood, right by the glittery window displays, I couldn't read the sign high up above us.

'All of you come here,' Mr Green began, once the last few had caught up. 'This shop here,' he said, pointing to the window display, 'is big, well big. When you get inside I want you to spread out. Go anywhere, but don't stay all together.' He looked around for a minute to check that none of the passing shoppers were listening. 'When it gets to closing, I want you to find somewhere to hide. Then stay there. The cameras won't be on tonight and the security

153

guard is. . . having a night off, all right? I'll try to be
back in the morning.'

With that Mr Green left us.

Would he have come back? I don't know. We didn't
get a chance to find out.

Chapter 22

I said earlier that I've never had a problem remembering things. Well there was one exception. I've never had a problem remembering things apart from the few hours after Mr Green sent us into that shop. I guess everything happened so quickly.

It's funny though. I've replayed it so many times in my mind, trying to see if there was anything else I could have or should have done, you'd think I'd remember it well. But it seems to get faster and fuzzier every time I think about it.

***

It wasn't long before it was closing time at the store. Me and Terri had stayed together as usual. We hid in the home department, under some beds. I remember the shop closing, the lights going off, the floors being swept, then mopped. After that it was quiet. I think I fell asleep. One moment it was silent, then the next I could hear people jumping across the beds, shouting and whooping. I looked out to see Ibby's trainers as he ran past.

I slid myself free of the bed and peered into the gloom. I could just make out rows of beds covered in white sheets. Terri appeared next to me. Then Jamal and Prince came bounding into view across the beds.

'Hey, Em!' Prince called. 'This is brilliant!'

'Don't you think we should be a bit quieter?' I asked.

Jamal echoed me in a squeaky voice, '*Don't you think we should be a bit quieter?* Why, you heard what Mr Green said, he's done something with the guard, there's no one here!'

Dwayne leapt towards us, shouting, 'Hello, we're jumping on the beds!'

Then everything happened really quickly. Kieran came running out of the darkness and jumped on to the bed that Prince was on. They were both laughing as they tumbled off the other side. They crashed into a glass case that held electrical stuff. Some lights came on, and a heartbeat later a piercing sound hit our ears.

'Run!' Jamal shouted over the screeching alarm.

And we ran. I grabbed Terri's hand and we all hurtled towards the exits. We found ourselves tumbling down the stairs just behind Jamal, Ibby and Dwayne. Kieran followed. We crashed into a fire exit at the bottom and out on to the street. If it was possible, the alarm sounded even louder on the street.

Down the road we could see flashing lights approaching, so we didn't stop running. We tore down the high street, then down another road. Jamal was in front, with Kieran puffing along behind. Terri was dragging at my hand but I didn't let go.

We ran until we found a bus-stop. We stopped there and looked back. No one was following us. We stood panting. I had my hands on my knees, head hanging down.

Then Jamal whispered, 'What happened to Prince?'

I stood up quickly and looked around. Where was Prince? Last time I'd seen him, he and Kieran had crashed into that glass cabinet.

'What happened to him, Kieran?' I asked, then noticed something even more disturbing than Prince's absence. Blood was streaked across Kieran's shirt. 'What happened?' I repeated.

Kieran was shrugging. 'I don't know,' he said slowly. 'We broke that glass, and then. . . I don't know.'

'Ah!' I shouted, not knowing what else to do. 'I'm going back.' I turned to run back the way we had come.

Terri grabbed my arm. 'You can't,' she whispered urgently. 'You'll get caught.'

'He's my brother! I've got to look after him.' I was staring at Terri, my anger at Kieran, my anger at Prince, my anger at Mr Green all directed at her.

'We'll... we'll get Mr Green.' Jamal sounded scared, not like him at all. 'He'll know what to do.' As Jamal finished speaking, a bus approached the bus-stop. 'Come on,' Jamal said and leapt on to the bus.

Everyone followed, Ibby, Kieran, Dwayne and Terri. I stood for a moment looking back down the street.

I was torn. What was the best thing I could do to help Prince? Stay and probably get caught, or go and maybe, just maybe, find some help from Mr Green.

'You getting on?' The bus driver's voice was gruff, like rustling paper.

***

Apparently Jamal knew where Mr Green lived. He had even been there a few times. We had to get on two more buses. Two more buses away from Prince. I spent the whole journey silent. Too angry and scared to speak.

I had let everyone down. I hadn't looked after Prince at all. He was all alone now.

It must have been almost midnight when we arrived at Mr Green's flat. It was really dark and the last bus had been almost empty, just us and an old man who kept shouting at no one.

Jamal rang the doorbell. We waited for a few minutes, then Jamal rang again. We heard some noises inside. Footsteps. We saw a light come on in the hallway. Then the door swung open.

'What the. . ! What are you doing here?' Mr Green was shouting and whispering at the same time.

None of us answered before Mr Green said, 'Get inside!' And he herded us all in. As soon as he had closed the door he grabbed Jamal by the collar. 'What are you bringing them all here for? I told you to keep your mouth shut.'

A woman called from a room further into the flat. 'Who is that?'

'No one. Just go to sleep, I'll be back in a bit,' Mr Green called back. He dragged Jamal by his collar through a doorway. We all followed. We were in a lounge. A big television took up most of one wall and there was a low table in the middle, covered in cans. It smelt weird.

Mr Green said again, 'What are you doing here?' He let go of Jamal's collar and pushed past us to shut the door into the hallway.

'It's Prince,' Jamal began. 'We were in that shop and an alarm went off and we ran. I guess all the others got away. I don't know, we haven't seen 'em, but we think Prince was hurt. He didn't. . . he's not with us.'

'Ah! You lot are useless!' Mr Green was shout-whispering again. He looked furious. 'What do you want me to do about it? If he's got caught I can't help him.'

All my hopes were pinned on Mr Green. But he was right, he couldn't help. He was using us, but what did he do for us? What did he do for Sastre? What would he do for Prince?

He was no longer magical to me. He didn't seem great. I wanted to be nowhere near him. But I still had nowhere else to go, no one to rely on and no one to trust.

I exploded. 'Go and get him!' I screamed. 'Get him out! That's what you do, isn't it? Get my brother back!'

It was then that the gun appeared. One minute he wasn't holding it and the next it was pointing right at me.

Mr Green didn't shout now. He just said slowly, 'Shut your mouth, boy.'

I could hear Terri crying, but I couldn't take my eyes off the gun to look at her or the others.

'You are lucky that I'm not kicking you out right now,' Mr Green continued. 'Sit down.' I heard rustling as the others sat down and a clunk as someone knocked over a can. 'Now!'

I realised I was still standing, fixated by the weapon, and I dropped down on to the floor.

'I'm going to sleep.' No one made a sound as Mr Green talked. The gun was still pointed at my head. 'You are not going to make a sound.' He looked round at the others. I still couldn't take my eyes off the gun. 'In the morning, we'll see if we can find the others, but now I'm going to sleep.' With his free hand he put his finger to his lips. 'Not one sound.'

He lowered the gun and turned to walk out of the door.

'No!' My brain said it but it came out of Jamal's mouth, and as he shouted, he jumped up and grabbed hold of the gun in Mr Green's hand.

Mr Green didn't let go. He swung round to face Jamal. Anger was painted across his face. Jamal was snarling as he tried to wrestle the gun from Mr Green. Mr Green pulled back and Jamal was nearly lifted off his feet. They whipped around the room, crashing into the table.

They were both pressed up against the wall when the gun swung out to one side. Then there was a deafening noise and everyone froze.

The gun dropped to the floor. Mr Green and Jamal had both let go and were staring towards the sofa. I followed their gaze. Terri's eyes were open. No sound was leaving her mouth and no tears escaped her eyes. A big red hole pierced her neck. Blood gushed out.

You didn't need to see the hole to tell that she

was dead. Just one look in her eyes would tell you that. There was no joy or fear or hope in those eyes. She wouldn't read to me again. She wouldn't fall asleep as I read. She'd never be a writer.

I felt sick.

Still no one moved.

Then my fear and anger took over. Anger at myself for not looking after Prince or Terri, and fear of what might have happened to my brother.

I was quick. As quick as my brother, lightning-fingers Prince.

I stood up and picked up the gun.

It was much heavier than I expected. I struggled to hold it steady, two feet out in front of my face. Heavy, cold and terrible. I had seen several guns, hundreds if you count those in films and on television, but I had never held one. I had certainly never pointed a gun at someone's face. I had never threatened to take away a person's life.

'Give me the piece, Emmanuel,' said Mr Green without a trace of hesitancy, as I stared at his face through the sights of a pistol. His slow, accented drawl resounded with the confidence of a man who was used to obedience. 'Give it to me, boy!'

My hands shook as my resolve began to break.

I couldn't kill him.

'You've killed her,' I whispered.

'I said give me the piece, Emmanuel.' Mr Green stepped towards me as I stepped round him.

I pushed the door open with my foot, still pointing the gun at Mr Green. I could feel hot tears pouring down my face. I walked backwards down the hall and Mr Green followed me. I took one hand off the gun and nearly dropped it. With my free hand I opened the front door, still looking at Mr Green.

Then I turned and ran. My tears became cold as the night air hit my face, and I threw the gun into a bush as I streamed down Mr Green's road.

I was more alone than I had ever been.

Chapter 23

The rest of that night was a blur. I didn't run far. I was exhausted and I didn't hear anyone come after me. I found myself wandering along empty roads. I didn't know what to do. Should I go back to the department store? Or to a police station? Maybe Prince was really hurt. I even considered phoning my uncle.

In the end, every option disappeared. I had been so used to following I had stopped paying attention to where Mr Green took us. I had no idea where the store was. I hadn't even paid attention to what buses Jamal had taken us on. Even if I could find a hospital, what would I say? And phoning my uncle wasn't really an option.

Tired of wandering I climbed over a locked park gate and sat on a bench. I sat there for a long time in the dark. Thinking and crying.

The sun rose while I sat and thought about home. A tiny, dusty, one-room house with my mum and dadda, where I watched a tiny, baby Prince grow up. A musty house, full, full of plants and just me and my brother. House after house where Prince had changed and I'd changed, where we'd been changed by what we did and the people we did it with. Home.

A few hours after it had got light, I began to notice the noise of cars on the roads. It was then that a man in a green uniform came walking down the path towards me. He had a green cap as well as a green uniform.

'Oi,' he said, 'you shouldn't be in here at night.'

I didn't answer. I got up and walked to the gate. It was open now. As I went out, I stuck my hands in my pockets. There was nothing in there but a screwed-up piece of paper. I pulled it out. It said, 'King's Church: Help is at hand.' It had an address and a phone number and a picture of some smiling people. I remembered where it had come from – SD, the wallet man.

As I read this tiny life-line, I knew what I needed.

I needed help. For a long time I had needed help. I couldn't do it alone, look after Prince, look after me, look after Terri. I needed help.

I finished reading. I looked up and, like magic, there was a church, right opposite the park gate. I walked straight over to it.

The church had a big wooden door. Not like an old-fashioned one. A new one with a glass panel and a metal button. It had a little sign that said *Press for attention*. I pressed the button.

Moments later a lady's voice came crackling out of a little speaker next to the button. 'Hello, St. John's.'

'Can you help me?' I said, and just like that my life of crime was over.

No more stealing. No more guns.

No more violence.

***

The people in St. John's kind of helped me. They invited me inside and asked me some questions. They gave me a drink in a plastic cup and some biscuits out of a big tin.

They made some phone calls and some other adults came. A man and a woman. They said they were from

Social Services. I didn't know what that meant.

They took me to some offices. They asked me lots and lots of questions. I asked some questions about Prince. They made some phone calls. They told me Prince was OK. They told me that I didn't need to worry.

'Some really nice people are looking after him,' they said. That made me cry for a little while. But it was the kind of crying that makes you feel better. Then they took me to a lady's house.

She was a big lady. And I mean big. She was called Esmerelda. She was from Africa too. We talked about that a bit.

I didn't stay with Esmerelda for long. She said that she only looked after children for a little while.

Social Services moved me to live with a lady called Alice. And that is where I live now, with Alice. She's quite old, but really strong. We have arm-wrestles and she normally wins. I think when I win it's because she lets me.

I have a pretty ordinary life now. I go to a new school. I play football. I have some friends. I keep up with the right programmes, but I don't listen to Lil' Legacy any more. I miss Asad and Ikram. I miss Terri. I miss Prince most of all.

Chapter 24

A few months ago, during the school holidays, Alice took me to the beach. We stayed for a week in a little, tiny house where you could see the sea from the top windows.

She asked me why I was so quiet all the time. I didn't know what to say. I didn't want to talk about everything that had happened. She asked if I wanted to write it down. That's when I started this. She bought me a big pad of paper. And by the sea, I wrote and wrote. Alice read some and told me to keep writing. So I have, and I've nearly finished now.

You've probably got a few questions that you'd like me to answer.

What happened to Mr Green and Jamal and the others?

I don't really know. I told the Social Services people as much as I knew about Mr Green, eventually. Everything that's written down here, really. I hope the gang are all safe. I hope that they all have their own Alice. Even Jamal. I think he needed someone to look after him most of all. And I hope that Mr Green has been put in prison for a very long time.

What happened to my uncle?

This I do know. About a week after we got back from that house by the sea, me and Alice were watching the news. Alice likes to watch it every day. There was a report about a big police raid. Something to do with drugs. Some men were being deported. Alice told me that this means they were being sent out of Britain to their own country. Then they showed pictures of their faces - and there, right in the middle of the screen, was my uncle.

What about my parents?

Here I have no idea. Maybe they will come and find me one day. Maybe not.

Probably the biggest question you have is what happened to my brother? What happened to Prince?

Here, I have a proper answer for you.

About a week ago, on a Saturday morning, I was reading in my room. Alice had bought me a copy of *Oliver Twist*. She said that I should try to read it again. She helps me with the hard bits. She bought me a dictionary too, that helps as well.

While I was reading, Alice knocked on the door. She always knocks.

'Come in,' I said.

She poked her head round the door, then came all the way in. As she sat down on my bed she said, 'How are you getting on with your book?'

'OK,' I replied.

She smiled a big smile at me and said, 'Good.' Then her smile got even bigger and she said, 'Something came in the post for you today, Emmanuel.'

My brow furrowed in surprise. I thought, who knew that I was here? Who would be writing to me?

She sat down on the bed next to me and placed a small, white envelope in my hands. The address was handwritten in a neat, flowing script. I tore open the top and pulled out a lined sheet of paper which had been folded a few times too many.

I looked up at Alice and her smile got even bigger, which didn't seem possible.

I unfolded and read the letter. It was in a different

handwriting to the address, big, unjoined-up writing.

Dear Emmanuel, my big brother,

I hope you get this. The people I live with have been helping me to find where you live now. They are nice. They are called Jubrel and Ruth. They said that I should write to you. I have written my address and my phone number on the top, so you could write back if you wanted to.

I wanted to write to you to say sorry. I was not always a good brother. I didn't listen to what you said sometimes. I hope I didn't let you down too much.

I also want to say thank you. You are the best big brother in the world. You looked after me and I love you Em. I miss you.

Please write back soon,

Your brother, Prince Anatole

PS Are you still a slow-coach?

I smiled at that last line, through the tears that were gathering in my eyes.

Alice touched me on the shoulder and said, 'I'd like us to go somewhere today, Emmanuel. I'd like to take you to see someone very special.'

'OK,' I said.

'Get your things together. You can bring your book. I'll meet you downstairs in... five minutes?'

'OK,' I said again.

'Oh, and bring your football,' she said as she left my room.

In the car I didn't ask where we were going, but I hoped.

We had driven for around half an hour when Alice said, 'Right, I think this is us.' We pulled into a road. There were big houses down one side of the road and a park on the other.

We pulled up outside a house with a red front door and a black knocker. I got out and looked up at the house, and there in the front window was an even bigger smile than Alice had given me earlier. A huge smile on the most familiar face that I know.

And for the first time since I had left Prince, I smiled.

I smiled back at my brother.

TOO MUCH TROUBLE

is the winner of the 2010
Frances Lincoln Diverse Voices
Children's Book Award

The Frances Lincoln Diverse Voices Children's Book Award was founded jointly by Frances Lincoln Limited and Seven Stories, in memory of Frances Lincoln (1945-2001) to encourage and promote diversity in children's fiction.

The Award is for a manuscript that celebrates cultural diversity in the widest possible sense, either in terms of its story or the ethnic and cultural origins of its author.

The prize of £1500, plus the option for Frances Lincoln Children's Books to publish the novel, is awarded to the best work of unpublished fiction for 8-12-year-olds by a writer aged 16 years or over, who has not previously published a novel for children. The winner of the Award is chosen by an independent panel of judges.

Please see the Frances Lincoln or Seven Stories website for further details.
www.franceslincoln.com
www.sevenstories.org.uk

seven
stories

The running and administration of the Frances Lincoln
Diverse Voices Children's Book Award is led by Seven
Stories, in Newcastle upon Tyne. Seven Stories is Britain's
children's literature museum. It brings the wonderful
world of children's books to life through lively exhibitions
and inspiring learning and events programmes. Seven
Stories is saving Britain's children's literature by building
a unique archive that shows how authors and illustrators
turn their thoughts and ideas into finished books of stories,
poems and pictures.

Seven Stories believes that children should be able to
choose books that reflect the lives of children from different
cultures in the world today. Frances Lincoln, in whose
memory the Award was founded, had an unswerving
commitment to finding talented writers who brought new
voices, characters, places and plots to children's books.

Arts
&Business

Frances Lincoln Limited and Seven Stories gratefully
acknowledge the support of Arts & Business for the
Frances Lincoln Diverse Voices Children's Book Award.

Tom Avery grew up in south-east London
with two big brothers and one little sister.
He followed in his father's footsteps by training
as a teacher at the University of Greenwich.
Whilst training, Tom ran a church youth club in
Lewisham, and then went on to teach in
Greenwich and Birmingham. He now works at
a diverse primary school in Camden Town,
London. Much of Tom's inspiration comes from
the pupils he has taught and the stories they have
shared, and much of his encouragement comes
from his wife and his mum, who has always
wanted him to be a writer. *Too Much Trouble*
is his first published book.
Tom lives with his wife, Chloe, and their
two sons, in Islington, London.